SINISTER

By

WRITERS ANONYMOUS

Note for Librarians: A cataloguing record for this book is available from Library and Archives Canada at www.collectionscanada.ca/amicus/index-e.html
ISBN 1-4120-9622-7

Printed in Victoria, BC, Canada. Printed on paper with minimum 30% recycled fibre. Trafford's print shop runs on "green energy" from solar, wind and other environmentally-friendly power sources.

TRAFFORD
PUBLISHING™
Offices in Canada, USA, Ireland and UK

Book sales for North America and international:
Trafford Publishing, 6E–2333 Government St.,
Victoria, BC V8T 4P4 CANADA
phone 250 383 6864 (toll-free 1 888 232 4444)
fax 250 383 6804; email to orders@trafford.com
Book sales in Europe:
Trafford Publishing (UK) Limited, 9 Park End Street, 2nd Floor
Oxford, UK OX1 1HH UNITED KINGDOM
phone 44 (0)1865 722 113 (local rate 0845 230 9601)
facsimile 44 (0)1865 722 868; info.uk@trafford.com
Order online at:
trafford.com/06-1378

10 9 8 7 6 5 4 3 2 1

"Thanks to Sam for inspiring us to create this book and thanks to Ingrid and Nikki for correcting it."

CONTENTS

SHINGAMI

By Trish Gibbs-Leake

I'm afraid of the dark.
Of something nameless,
Wordless
Crawling slowly up behind
And leaning on my shoulder.

A cold and clammy numbness
Shifting, sliding past unnoticed
And soaking down both arms
Until I try to lift them,
To push away the smother-fear
Pressed against my mouth and nose
And intimately sucking life and breath
From inside me.

Shingami: The Japanese Angel of Death.

Sinister

PUPPET PARODY

By Nicolette Coleman

A 'puppet' is any controlled character, whether formed by a shadow, strings or by the use of a glove...

"Jasmine, you are looking up at the ceiling! Make him look at his audience."

"OK." Jasmine moved the puppet so that he was looking down over the curtain towards an imaginary audience. I smiled at her, rubbing my arm, which was aching from being held upright for so long.

"Right, let's go through the song one more time before we finish," Bob called. Gratefully we brought our arms down, shaking them out a little to restore some circulation. Turning towards the back wall we held our arms out, waiting for the music to begin, then made the puppets walk up invisible stairs to start the song.

"I love your new puppet," Jasmine said as we packed away the curtains.

"Thanks. She only arrived in this morning's post. I like her too, I think she looks a bit like me with her blonde curly hair. Don't you think? What do you think I should call her? I was thinking of Joy."

"Yes, she is like you. Same big smile too." Jasmine laughed, her head on one side. "Yep. Joy is a good name, she's got a lovely joyful smile on her face. Where did you get her from? She's not the same as the ones Bob has."

"From the Internet. I know most of the sites that sell puppets are really expensive, but I did a big search, for dolls as well as puppets. The site I got her from don't call them puppets, they call them life-like figurines. They send the puppets from Zambia. They are much cheaper than Bob's puppets, but I think the quality is at least as good. Feel how soft her skin and hair are. She's almost human!"

I drove home from the church with Joy strapped into the passenger seat beside me. I was thrilled with my new friend. I had longed for a puppet of my own ever since joining the puppet troupe two years ago. Originally I joined them as a way to pass the time after my fiancé, John, had decided he couldn't go through with our wedding. As if marriage to me was a trial he was expected to endure. Ashamed of being deserted, and unwilling to show my grief to my friends and colleagues, I had decided I needed to keep myself busy, to fill up the hours which used to be filled with John. It had worked to a certain extent, although the nights were still filled with long, dark, empty hours. I still felt a great longing for someone of my own. Someone who would love me best of all. If all had gone according to plan, by now John and I would have been married, hopefully with a baby to love and care for. I longed so much for a baby.

As a small child I had pestered my mother to have another child, a baby who I could look after. She had laughed at me, telling me; "You'll have a baby of your own one day. Lots of them probably. Then you'll have more than enough to keep you busy. Now run along and play."

I stopped outside my flat, grateful that for once I could park within walking distance instead of at the other end of the road. I lifted Joy into my arms and took her indoors. It was warmer inside than out, as I had left the heating set low. Coming home to a cold flat seemed a particularly lonely thing to do, I had always thought. My mother thought me a spendthrift, but I always set the heating to come on half an hour before I was due home. That way I felt welcomed.

"Ruby! Ruby!" I called out as I walked up the stairs, and was quickly rewarded by the sound of paws pattering across the hall, and the sinuous feel of the cat winding her way between my legs as I walked into the lounge.

Tonight I did not feel as alone as normal, as I had my new companion, Joy, with me. I sat her on the sofa while I made a cup of drinking chocolate. She smiled up at me as I turned on the television and settled myself next to her, patting her on the head.

"We'll just watch the news before bed, Joy. I expect you're tired after your busy evening." I pulled her closer to my side. I imagined this would be how it would feel to have a small child snuggled up to me on the sofa. A warm feeling of satisfaction filled me, and I wiggled my toes happily as I sipped at the hot chocolate.

The cat was on the mat in front of the gas fire, her hackles raised, as she glared at Joy. I laughed, and rubbed her fur, leaning down towards her. "Silly old Ruby! I can have another friend as well as you. I'm sure you, and Joy, will soon get used to each other." I tried to get her to sit with me on the sofa, but she stubbornly remained on the mat.

After a warm bath I climbed into bed, pulling the duvet up around my chin, but I was unable to settle. Was Joy feeling alone and left out, in the living room? What if somebody broke into the flat and stole her while I slept? Nobody but me knew how much less she had cost than the usual brand of puppets. She could be sold for quite a lot of money. I got out of bed and tiptoed into the front room, where Joy was sitting as I'd left her, still smiling at me. I picked her up, holding her close as I made my way back to the bedroom. She could sit on the chair by the window. That way she would feel safe, and I could see that she was happy. I tucked a cushion behind her for support and comfort. "Goodnight Joy," I said, kissing her on the cheek.

Back in bed I snuggled down again, much more at peace now that Joy was here.

Yawning and rubbing my eyes as I awoke the next morning, I looked up and the first thing I saw was Joy, grinning away at me.

"Morning Joy," I mumbled, giving her a pat on my way to the bathroom. As I combed my hair I noticed a small rash on my neck. I hoped I was not allergic to whatever Joy was made of. I pulled the collar of my blouse up to hide it, before heading for the kitchen and breakfast. I felt weary, as if I had not slept well, although I couldn't remember waking in the night. Vague dreamy images flitted at the edges of my memory. I sighed. It would be a long day at work if I began the day feeling so tired. I brought Joy into the kitchen with me while I ate breakfast, sitting her on the spare chair opposite mine. She continued to smile at me as she watched me eat. I felt a bit mean, eating while she watched me, so I put an empty plate and cup in front of her. "Breakfast!" I said, and could have sworn she winked in response, but it must have been the movement of shadows in the kitchen. I found myself wishing that I had a highchair to sit her in, and considered looking for a second-hand one in the local paper. But as I reflected on it, I decided it probably wasn't such a good idea. I didn't have very many visitors to my flat, but those who did come might think I was a bit barmy if they saw a highchair in the kitchen.

Ruby sat on the floor, slurping disgustingly from her bowl, never taking her eyes from Joy. She must be jealous, I thought, as it was normally just her and me eating together. I stroked her soft fur on my way out of the room, and was rewarded with a soft purring.

Coming home from the office that afternoon I felt heartened at the thought of Joy waiting for me. She could sit and watch as I had my dinner. Perhaps I would give her her own plate, as I had done at breakfast. I let myself into the flat, calling out; "I'm home!"

While Ruby wound herself around my legs, I walked into the lounge, where I found Joy sitting on the sofa, looking for all the world as if she had been watching television. I picked her up and hugged her to me. Walking to the kitchen I was stopped by a strange thought — hadn't I left Joy in the kitchen that morning when I went to work? No. I must have forgotten where I left her — she could hardly walk into the lounge, could she? I noted that Ruby had run off into the kitchen when I picked Joy up. I found her sitting by her bowl, glowering at me. I made sure to put Joy on a chair before squatting down to pet Ruby, who quickly resumed her usual happy purring when I stroked her.

When I went to bed that night I again sat Joy on the bedroom chair, this time covering her with a fleece blanket, as the night was so cold. As I began to drift off to sleep I thought I heard a soft voice from across the room, whispering something I couldn't quite catch. Quietly I sat up in bed, listening for any sound. All was silent. I was about to lie down again, convinced it had been my imagination, when I heard it again; "I'm cold. Emma, I'm cold." Such a faint voice, calling from the shadows. I leant forwards, straining into the darkness, to see what was there. A shadow moved near the window, and I jumped. "Who's there?" I whispered, my voice a pathetic quiver.

10

"It's me. I'm cold Emma. Let me get in bed with you." The voice trickled out of the dark, so gentle and quiet. I leaned over and turned on the bedside light, blinking in the sudden harsh light. There was nobody in the room, nothing was moving except my shadow on the wall. I looked over at the chair by the window, and there sat Joy, smiling and smiling at me. The blanket had fallen from her shoulders, and she looked so cold sitting there that I leapt out of bed, picked her up and brought her into bed with me. I turned off the light and lay down, hugging Joy to me, trying to stop the shakes, which pulsed through my limbs. She felt soft and comforting, like a big teddy bear. I stroked her soft hair, and tumbled down and down into sleep.

The shrill of the alarm shocked me awake what felt like minutes later. I groaned as I reached to turn it off. I felt exhausted, my limbs heavy and slow. My head and neck ached, and my eyes were gritty and sore. I stood under the shower for a long time, letting the hot water release the tension in my neck and shoulders. I must be getting the flu, or some kind of virus, I supposed. I took a couple of aspirin with my breakfast, hoping they would stave off the pains for a few hours.

I arrived at work heavy headed and ill tempered, wishing I'd stayed home in bed. Everything was a struggle, and I found myself unable to manage even the simplest task. At lunchtime a few of my colleagues invited me to the pub, but I turned them down, and sat at my desk with a limp sandwich and a cup of soup, longing for the afternoon to end.

As I tried to make myself eat, I noticed Mark, the office heartthrob, wandering towards my desk. He sat on the corner of the desk and smiled down at me.

"Not off to the pub with the others then?" His eyes crinkled as he smiled at me, and I felt myself flushing under his gaze.

"No. Not feeling up to drinking today. I think I might be coming down with something." I looked down at the desk, picking at the crust of my sandwich.

"That's a shame," Mark replied, "I don't suppose you feel up to a drink out tonight then?"

I struggled to answer. Was he suggesting a date? Or a drink with friends? Having no idea, I shook my head; "No, sorry, not tonight. Think I'll have an early night. Some other time perhaps?"

"Sure." He smiled and strolled back to his own desk, lifting his hand in a wave as he went. I sat there, scratching at my sore neck, going over our conversation in my mind.

The working day finally came to an end, and I drove back through the rush-hour traffic, trying my best to concentrate. There were more cars about than normal, and as I pulled into my road I could see that I would be unable to park anywhere near the flat.

Driving slowly up the road I scanned for a space big enough to park in, finally spying a small gap some thirty houses up from mine. Backing up, I at length managed to park the car, squeezing it in between two others. I closed the door and began trudging back towards my flat, wishing I had not worn such high heels that day, as the balls of my feet burned with pain.

At the gate I stopped, looking upwards in surprise. The light was on in my lounge. There was no way I would have left it on that morning. I was sure it was already daylight when I left for work. Wasn't it?

With shaking fingers I unlocked the door, and tentatively started up the stairs. Would I find a burglar waiting for me? Or a ransacked flat? I tiptoed up, wondering why I was being so quiet when I of all people had the right to be here. At the top of the stairs I hesitated, looking to right and left. There was no noise, and no signs of having been burgled. Feeling braver I ventured forwards, until I reached the lounge door. Hesitating for just a second, I flung the door open, jumping back at the same time in case somebody leapt out at me. But there was nobody there. The light was on, and Joy was sitting on the sofa, smiling up at me. I was sure that she turned her head towards me as I entered the room, and a leaf-shake of terror ran up my legs. Was I going mad, imagining things? A puppet can't turn its head without a hand inside it. Oh God! Was there someone in the room, behind Joy? But as I shakily looked around I realised the impossibility of this, as Joy was sat on the sofa, with nowhere behind her for anybody to hide.

"The lights are on, but no one's home," I found myself muttering, half hysterically. I sat down beside Joy, absent-mindedly pulling her on to my lap and stroking her hair as I waited for my heartbeat to slow.

As I calmed down, I realised that Ruby hadn't rushed to greet me as she usually did. I stood up, dropping Joy back onto the sofa as I called, "Ruby? Ruby?" and toured the flat. She was not on my bed — her usual haunt when I was not there to chase her off. The kitchen door was ajar, and I paused before walking in. As I felt for the light my foot slipped on something wet on the floor. I looked down, and saw to my horror that the floor was slick with blood. I stood trembling in the doorway, looking around the small room, calling to Ruby in a whisper. And then I spied her, lying flat on the floor under the table, her legs stiff, her eyes closed, and her neck (oh God! Her neck!) slashed open, the inside of her throat wide, wet and glistening in the light.

I sank to my knees, sobs catching in my throat, bile rising to choke me. Tentatively I reached out to touch Ruby, but the cold, damp, lifeless feel of her fur repelled me. Who could have done such a thing to my lovely cat? Who would hurt a helpless animal? Then I remembered the light in the lounge, and stumbled back there to pick up the phone and dial 999.

When the police arrived, I showed them my poor Ruby, telling them about finding the light on when I returned home. They asked a lot of questions about who had access to my flat, and took some fingerprints. I remembered that John still had a key to the flat, and foolishly mentioned the fact to the police, who then bombarded me with questions about the state of our relationship. I assured them that John and I no longer had a relationship, and had not spoken to each other for over a year. I promised them that he would have no reason to kill Ruby, especially after such a long absence, but felt they were disinclined to believe me. They asked if I wanted them to take Ruby and have her disposed of, and I found myself nodding, unable to bear the thought of touching that body again, or the difficulty of finding somewhere to bury her.

Getting ready for bed I automatically took Joy into the bed with me, hugging her to my chest like a comfort blanket, sobbing into her soft hair. "You're my only friend now," I heard myself whisper. It took me a while to fall asleep. I lay there in the dark, my thoughts skittering about, tensing at every real or imagined noise. Eventually I began to relax, and my limbs became heavier.

"Don't worry, Emma, I'm here to look after you," a soft voice crooned in my ear. But I was too sleepy and simply pulled Joy tighter into my arms. As I fell into sleep I felt a soft scratching at my neck. I tried to move, to pull away from whatever was touching me, but I was unable, paralysed as I was, with tiredness.

The night passed slowly, as in my dreams I felt myself pushed and pulled about, my neck scratched and stabbed at, and my whole body felt as though it was being pulled through a mangle. I swam wearily through the darkness, aware with a tiny part of my mind that I was wishing for morning to come.

When the alarm finally shrilled, I struggled towards the surface of consciousness, reaching groggily for the button on the clock. Sitting up I put my head in my hands, leaning forwards to rest my elbows on my knees. After a few minutes I tried to stand up, but my legs were like jelly, and I felt empty inside. Rubbing at my neck, I turned to look at Joy, who lay quietly on the pillow, grinning up at me, a red stain around her mouth. Worried, I leant over her. What on earth could she have got on her face during the night?

As I moved my hand towards her, I swear she moved away from me. I sat there, shaking. Was I finally going mad? When John left me he had made some comment about my living in a fantasy world. I had assumed that he was referring to the fact that I wanted to get married and have his babies. But could he have meant something more? Was there something weird about me? I had often felt that people didn't really like me very much, but... But what? As far as I was aware I had never hallucinated before. But how would I know? How do you know if a hallucination is real, or simply a joke from your fevered brain? I leapt up from the bed, suddenly wanting to be away from Joy.

Sobbing with fear and grief as I recalled the events of the previous evening, I dressed quickly, leaving the flat without eating any

14

breakfast. I was anxious to get away, to shut the door behind me and return to the more normal world of work. I realised that I was still crying, when I noticed the man in the next car staring at me at the traffic lights, and hastily brushed my hand across my eyes, trying to summon a smile.

I hunched down behind my computer when I arrived at work, not wishing to talk to anybody. I wanted to tell them about Ruby, but knew I was incapable of telling the story without breaking down. I tried to work, pushing papers around my desk, and wishing I could lose myself in busyness, as I had done in the past.

At 11 o'clock I realised that I had eaten or drunk nothing since lunch the day before. I would go to the coffee bar round the corner, and buy myself a coffee and a Danish pastry I decided. Reaching down to get my bag, I caught sight of my chest. With embarrassed dismay I realised that I was wearing my teddy-printed winceyette pyjama top over a pinstriped skirt. I must have forgotten to finish dressing in my haste to leave the flat this morning. How was I going to get out of the office without anybody noticing? Hot with embarrassment, I dared to look up, just in time to see Kelly and Janice exchanging amused glances, and I knew that they had seen. I stood up as fast as I could; grabbing my coat and hugging my bag to my chest in a vain attempt to hide my pyjama top, and rushed towards the door. As I hurried out, I realised that I was also not wearing a bra, and was horribly aware of my breasts wobbling up and down as I ran.

I headed straight for my car, shutting the door and sealing myself inside my own private space. My hands shook so much I was unable to turn the key in the ignition at first. I made myself stop and take a few deep breaths before trying again. I drove as carefully as I was able, until I reached my road, where I found to my relief that there was a space right by my front door. As I was about to get out of the car I saw that my next door neighbour, elderly Mrs. Briggs, was walking towards me. I huddled down as far as possible towards the floor of the car, pulling my head into my chest. I stayed that way until my back began to complain at the unnatural position I had put it in. Peering up I saw with relief that Mrs. Briggs was no longer in sight, so I hurried out of the car and up my front path, hardly drawing breath until I was inside the flat, with the door locked behind me. I sat down on the bottom step, sobbing into my hands; my legs shaking so hard I was afraid to attempt the stairs.

Eventually I pulled myself up and made my way up to my bedroom, where I lay on the bed, too exhausted and demoralised to move. I must have fallen asleep, because I knew nothing more until I was woken by the phone ringing. It was dusk, and I stumbled as I hurried towards the lounge. I picked up the phone, to find my boss, Pete, on the other end.

"Are you OK Emma?" He asked. "You disappeared before lunch, and nobody has heard from you since. We were worried about you."

"I'm so sorry," I found myself stuttering, "I don't feel at all well. I came home to get some painkillers and I must have fallen asleep. So sorry."

"Don't worry then. Look it's the weekend now. Take care of yourself, and we'll see you next week. Are you sure you'll be all right?" I could hear the puzzled concern in his voice, and hurried to reassure him that I would be fine after a rest. I had been an exemplary employee for the past ten years, and I realised that Pete was genuinely worried about me. I managed to finish the phone call, and hung up. I sat there for a while, too dispirited to move. I was beginning to wonder just what was really wrong with me. This was more than a virus — I had never before forgotten to get dressed properly. I felt so lethargic and hopeless, as if all my life's blood had been drained away.

What I needed was vitamins, I decided suddenly, pushing myself to my feet and heading for the kitchen. I knew I hadn't been eating properly this week, and I ought to take more care of myself. There was some orange juice in the fridge, and I poured a large glass, which I drank straight down, before pouring another, all the while keeping my eyes averted from the part of the kitchen where I had found Ruby. Rooting through the fridge I found some rather limp mushrooms and peppers, and an onion in the cupboard. I threw together a small stir fry, which I forced myself to eat, sitting at the table with a third glass of juice. I could get through this if I looked after myself by eating sensibly and not thinking about bad things. I picked up an apple from the bowl on the worktop, and carried it through to the lounge, determined to try and eat it later. That was the way normal, sane people, would behave, wasn't it?

I pulled the curtains shut and turned on the television, clicking on a table lamp before settling myself on the sofa. I stared blankly at the screen without paying it any real attention, turning an apple around and around in my hands. I had a vague feeling that something was missing. Was there something I ought to be doing? Too tired to think properly, I sat, half dozing.

"Emma. Emma, where are you?" The soft voice brought me back to full consciousness with a jerk, and I sat up suddenly, the apple falling from my hand to roll across the carpet, settling on the rug where my Ruby used to sit. Who had called me? I sat as still as I could, making no noise, using the remote control to silence the television. Had somebody really called me? Or was I imagining things again? I could feel the press of my heart thumping against my ribs, and my pulse throbbing in my ears was the only sound in the room.

"EMMA!" The voice shrieked through the flat, startling me so that I found myself leaping to my feet, shaking all over, needing to steady myself on the wall.

"Who's there?" I called, my voice a small tremble in the room.

"Emma! Come and get me, come on, you know what to do." The voice was quieter now, soothing and cajoling, and I found myself drawn towards it, tiptoeing out into the hall and heading towards the bedroom. I pushed the door open, not bothering with the light, as the brightness from the hall softly illuminated the room. Joy was sitting on the bed where I had left her that morning. Her face seemed to shine in the half-light, a gentle gleam coming from her dark button eyes. Her face was turned towards me. As I stared at her, her mouth opened and she spoke; "Why didn't you come to me Emma? You know I can make you feel better. Come on, come to me."

I stood frozen in the doorway, watching her mouth move, seeing how her lips opened and closed so much more naturally than when I was controlling her. But who, or what, was controlling her now?

17

"Come on Emma, you know you want me to comfort you," she appealed to me.

I found that, against my own volition, I was walking towards the bed. I sat on the edge of the mattress, cautiously reaching out my hand towards Joy. Her little hand reached towards mine, holding on to my fingers with surprising strength. I lay my head down on the pillow, lacking the will to do anything else. I felt Joy reach out and pull me into her embrace, and let my head fall to rest against her soft shoulder. She murmured soothingly into my ear, and I began to drift back to sleep. As I dozed I felt her push my hair away from my neck, and gently, so gently, sink her teeth into my flesh. What did anything matter any more? I let myself go.

Later I half woke to find it was morning. I tried to raise my weary head from the pillow, but Joy pulled me back again, stroking my heavy shoulders, and I again let go of my defences. The weekend drifted by in a warm haze. I was aware of very little, other than Joy's constant, soothing presence, and the softness of my bed. I thought I heard the phone ring a few times, and perhaps the doorbell too, but they were just impressions on the edge of my consciousness, and did not penetrate my mind's fog.

The alarm trilled near my ear, and I managed to force myself awake, struggling to sit up. It must be Monday morning, and somehow I needed to go to work, or at the very least ring them to let them know I would not be in.

As I tried to sit up I heard a noise in the bathroom, and then the bedroom door swung open. In the doorway stood Joy. She seemed taller and more solid than before. She was wearing one of my dresses, and her hair was pulled back the way I always wore my hair for work. My silver cross necklace sat on her chest, and the matching earrings swung from her ears. If I hadn't known better I would have thought I was watching myself in a mirror. Watching me all the time, she sat on the chair and pulled on my brown boots.

As I tried weakly to speak she walked towards me, stopping at the dressing table to pick up my glasses and perch them on her nose.

"What, what are you doing? What is happening?" I asked, my

voice small and weak. I felt as fragile and floppy as a rag doll, and it was hard to make my voice detectable.

Joy stood over me for a moment, then leant down towards me, put her hand on my chest and oh so gently pushed me, causing me to fall back against the pillows.

"Who's the puppet now?" she asked, her smile a cruel smirk. "I'll be late back tonight, Mark's taking me out to dinner. Don't wait up." And she left, her laugh a heartless echo in the bedroom.

I wanted to get up and go after her. This wasn't really happening, things like this didn't happen in real life. But I was unable to move. It seemed the stuffing had all been knocked out of me.

I lay there, watching through a gap in the curtains as the sun moved around the sky. What was I going to do? I needed to get out of here, to get some help from somebody who would believe me. The more I thought about it, the more I realised that I would have a great deal of trouble explaining myself to anybody. My story sounded ridiculous even to me.

At last I managed to find the strength to leave the bed, and headed for the kitchen. If, as I supposed, Joy had been drinking my blood to make her more like me, then I needed to rehydrate my body, and get some nourishment into me. I found that there was still some orange juice in the fridge, and I drank straight from the carton, leaning against the fridge for support. There were some eggs on the bottom shelf. I took them out of their packet, dropping them into a bowl in order to scramble them in the microwave. The sight and smell of them made me gag, but I made myself continue, dropping two slices of wholemeal bread into the toaster as the eggs cooked. When it was all cooked I slopped the eggs onto the toast, grated some cheese on the top, then forced myself to swallow the lot. I sat, determined to let the food nourish me. As I remained in the chair, I suddenly remembered that when people gave blood they were given tea and sweet biscuits afterwards. Well, that was what I would have too. As I clicked on the kettle I realised that tea and biscuits were also the bygone remedy for shock. Well, I thought, I have certainly had enough shocks this week.

Once the tea and biscuits were finished I ran myself a bath. I did not feel strong enough yet to stand in the shower. I lay in the warm scented water until it began to cool, pondering my options. I had to admit that over the years I had become somewhat reclusive, and this left me with no really close friends to talk to. My colleagues were just that, colleagues. OK, we occasionally went to the pub together, but there was nobody in the office I would really call a friend. Pete was a good boss, and I think he cared about me as much as anyone, but if I told him what had happened to me he would quietly contact the firm's psychologist to arrange an appointment.

Mark was becoming more of a friend, but Joy had said she had a date with him that night. What on earth would he think if I rang him and said, "Don't go out tonight. That's not me, it's a puppet!" he would run a mile. My mother would be no help. She would just say something inane like, "That's nice dear. Now don't you work too hard."

I had to get help and get out of the flat before Joy came back tonight. I dried myself on a large fluffy towel, rubbing some warmth back into my frigid skin. Dressing for warmth in jeans and a T-shirt, with a thick fleece over the top, I returned to the kitchen, where I made myself drink some more tea and eat a few more biscuits. "Nourishment. Nourishment," I kept muttering to myself.

The phone rang, a harsh jangling in the quiet afternoon, and I spilled tea down my fleece. I stumbled towards the phone, wiping my front with a tea towel as I went. Reaching for the phone my hand wavered. Who would it be? What was I going to say to them? I picked up the receiver. "Hello?"

"Oh, Emma, I'm so glad I caught you, I thought you might still be at the office. It's Jasmine."

"Jasmine. Oh, hello." This was a surprise. Jasmine and I hardly ever spoke outside of the puppet troupe meetings. I wondered if she was calling to chastise me for missing the last meeting.

"Emma, there's something I really need to talk to you about. I don't suppose I could come round to see you now, could I?"

I hesitated. I needed to talk to someone, but was Jasmine the one? But as this thought flitted through my mind, another followed it;

perhaps Jasmine was meant to phone me. The timing was pretty amazing.

"Come round Jasmine," I replied. "I'm here."

I put the kettle on again as I waited for Jasmine, and put a few biscuits out on a plate. The doorbell rang far sooner than I expected, and I lurched down the stairs, opening the door to let Jasmine in.

"You were quick," I said.

"I know. I was at the end of the road, hoping you would agree to see me." Jasmine's eyes were huge in her tiny face, and there was a set line to her mouth. She looked at me, her mouth opening into a surprised 'O'. "Gosh Emma, have you been ill? You look so thin and white."

I motioned her up the stairs and into the kitchen, where I poured tea, whilst deciding how much to tell her.

"Emma, it's only just over a week since I last saw you. What has happened?"

I looked at her. Jasmine had never given me any reason to doubt her, and I had never heard her say an unkind thing about anybody. "Tell me why you wanted to see me first," I countered.

Her face crumpled, and for a moment I thought she might cry, but she took a deep breath and sat up straight.

"Please don't think I'm silly and superstitious, will you?" I shook my head, wondering what was coming next. "I thought I might buy myself a puppet like your Joy," she continued, and I felt my heart plummet. I didn't want this to happen to Jasmine. I don't know what showed on my face as I thought this, but Jasmine looked alarmed, her eyes widening. "Well anyway, I looked for the website you told me about, but I kept getting an error message, so I did a search for similar site names, and I found a whole page of information about the puppet makers. Lots of people have written in with complaints and worries about the site." Jasmine looked up at me, gauging my reaction. I nodded, to afraid to speak, so she proceeded; "Emma, lots of people say that the puppet makers are really making voodoo dolls. They are as big as puppets, but they have had a spell put on them. I couldn't understand everything, but it was all to do with witchcraft. Oh

Emma, I've been so worried about you!"

I reached a shaky hand towards Jasmine, tears of relief running down my face. Jasmine rushed around the table and put her arms around my trembling shoulders. Unable to speak I just nodded and nodded at her. She understood what I was trying to convey and held me tighter, crying with me.

At last I was able to pull away and blow my nose. Hesitantly I began to speak, but then the words began to pour from me, a gushing of relief, and I watched Jasmine cry as I told her my story. When I had finished she walked over and held my hand.

"We need to get you out of here before Joy comes back," she said urgently, and I looked up at the clock. It was after seven, and Joy could be back any time. I stood up, flustered by panic, but Jasmine dragged me into the bedroom, pulling open the wardrobe and drawers. "What do you need to take for the next few days?" she asked, and I quickly chose some clothes and toiletries, shoving them into an overnight bag. Grabbing my handbag we dashed for the stairs, blundering down them two at a time.

Jasmine's car was parked over the road, and we locked ourselves in. As she started the engine and pulled away Jasmine laughed. "Anyone would think we'd gone mad," she said.

"I thought I had. Oh, thank you for coming to rescue me!"

"That's OK. I couldn't just do nothing once I found out about the puppets. But we need to decide what to do about Joy. You can't just leave her roaming around town, masquerading as you."

We went to Jasmine's flat, where she cooked us dinner, and we sat and deliberated over a bottle of wine.

"You know, without my blood to drink from, Joy won't have much strength, will she? Perhaps if we do nothing, just leave her for a few days she might become so weak that we can get rid of her somehow." I wasn't sure if I was grasping at straws, but could think of nothing else.

Jasmine nodded. "You might be right. You can stay here for a few days if you like, while we see what happens." I thanked her, touched that she was so keen to help me, when I knew I had never been much of a friend to her. Ashamed, I recalled the times she had invited me to go to the pub with her, but I had refused, preferring my own miserable company.

I slept well that night, bolstered by Jasmine's friendship, and the knowledge that with all the good food I had eaten that day my body was beginning to repair itself. Already I could feel some of my strength returning.

The next morning Jasmine drove to my home, where she sat outside, waiting to see if Joy emerged. When she returned her eyes were red and puffy and her face was blotchy.

"What happened?" I demanded. Jasmine sat down and looked up at me.

"She looks so like you!" She said, her voice little more than a whisper. "I was just so shocked, it was as if I was looking at you going to work. She even drove your car! I feel quite sick Emma."

I hugged her, aware of the shock she was feeling, which was nothing to the shock I had felt on realising what had been happening to me. Jasmine phoned in sick to work, and I had to admit that she did look unwell. We spent the day resting, watching daytime television and drinking coffee. At 4:30 Jasmine got ready to go out again. "I need to see her come home again Emma," she said.

She was gone for a long two hours, and I fretted, wondering what had happened to her. Had Joy spotted her and done something unspeakable? I kept myself busy cooking dinner, and when Jasmine finally walked through the door it was to be greeted by the smell of shepherd's pie wafting through the flat. I looked at her carefully, and was relieved to see that she looked a lot happier than she had this morning.

"It's working!" she exclaimed as I raised my eyebrows in query. "When she came back tonight she looked awful. Much less human. I don't really know how to explain, but she looked floppier somehow."

"More like a puppet?" I queried.

"That's it! More like a puppet! What she has done to you must somehow be reversing as she has no access to human blood!"

We ate our dinner with a faint sense of celebration hanging in the air. I was afraid to believe that my nightmare might soon be over, but felt full of hope. We sat watching a film on television, sharing a bottle of wine, and chatting like old friends. I was wondering why I had kept Jasmine at arm's length for so long. She was such a lovely, generous person, and I was lucky to have her on my side.

The following morning Jasmine again left the flat. She did not return until almost 11 o'clock, by which time I was almost climbing the walls.

"She hasn't left the flat!" She cried, almost before she had got inside the door. "I think this could be it!"

In the afternoon Jasmine drove me home. I opened the front door, and we crept up the stairs, listening for any sound. The flat was silent. I stood on the landing, unsure of which room to try first, then I heard a faint sound from the bedroom. Beckoning Jasmine I pushed open the door. Joy was lying in my bed, her face turned towards me. Her face had the texture of felt, and her hair looked like nothing so much as a hank of wool. Her button eyes were dull and lacklustre. As I watched she opened her mouth, trying to speak, but no sound emerged. I heard Jasmine gasp beside me as she watched.

I walked towards the bed. "Who's the puppet now?" I murmured. I opened my handbag, and took out the large carrier bag I had hidden in there. Pulling back the covers, I quickly lifted Joy into the bag, being careful not to let her mouth anywhere near my neck.

I could feel her struggling feebly as I tied some string around the top of the bag. Jasmine looked like a rabbit caught in headlights. "Come on," I urged as I headed for the front door, "Don't get scared now."

Jasmine followed me quickly down the stairs, her hand resting lightly on my shoulder. "I didn't really understand," she whispered behind me, "When I heard her speak!" Her voice trailed off. I reached up and patted her hand before opening the front door and peering out. I was gratified that the road was empty for once, and we hurried towards Jasmine's car, once in the car she headed towards her flat. The traffic was getting heavier as the mothers came out to collect their children from school. I could feel Joy trying to struggle free in the bag at my feet. I was tempted to kick her, but couldn't bring myself to do it. I simply placed my booted foot on the top of the bag, which seemed to give her the correct message.

Finally we arrived back at Jasmine's flat, where we headed straight for the garden. At the very end of the grounds was an incinerator bin, almost full with autumn leaves and dead plants. Jasmine and I stood for a moment looking at each other, summoning up the courage to do what we had to do. From her pocket Jasmine took a box of matches, then determinedly strode forwards and set light to the leaves. It took a few moments before the fire took hold, and I was afraid that our plan wouldn't work. Gently Jasmine blew on the sparks until the flames grew in size and hue.

Once it was fully alight I stepped forward, the carrier bag held out in my hands. I could feel Joy moving inside still, and it gave me a queasy feeling, as though I was about to kill a child.

"Go on," Jasmine spurred me on, and I dashed forwards and thrust the wiggling bag deep into the flames. Standing back I watched as the flames overtook the bag, melting the plastic. For a horrible moment Joy's face was exposed, her mouth bared in a rictus of anger and pain, and then it was gone, swallowed up by orange flames. A huge screech rent the air, and Jasmine and I put our hands over our ears. Then, as we looked, a plume of sickly green smoke lifted up from the incinerator. It hovered over us for a moment, and a face was visible in the fumes for just a moment, looking down at us with pure hatred. Then, with a final screech, it was gone, and the air was filled with nothing more than the ordinary stench of bonfire.

We stood a while longer, just to be sure, then went back inside the flat, where Jasmine produced a bottle of sparkling wine. "I've been saving it for a special occasion," she said, "and I think this will do." We raised our glasses, "to freedom from fear", and emptied them in one mouthful. Spluttering and laughing we hugged each other.

"I can't thank you enough," I told Jasmine. "You really have saved my life. How can I ever repay you?"

Jasmine smiled at me. "There is one thing you can do for me." I nodded, willing her on. "You can move in here with me. I get lonely, and this flat is too big for one person. Anyway, I think you need someone to keep you out of trouble." My eyes stung, and I could do nothing more than nod and smile a watery smile. Jasmine refilled our glasses, and then raised hers in a final toast; "To friendship."

TOYS AT NIGHT

By Trish Gibbs-Leake

I sat and rocked my crying child and saw her room anew
And recognised the things that look like monsters when you're two

The mobile's swoop to get at her, the dolls' house window — eyes,
The green frog hanging on the wall was now a huge fat fly.
Her fluffy toys all sitting up, the darkness made afraid —
They were a massive black thing advancing on her bed.

At last I saw and understood the monsters and bad dreams,
And realised that being good's much harder than it seems.

Then I remembered someone else who ran through darkened gloom,
Too fast for anyone to catch — to Mummy's and Daddy's room.

So when she stumbles to our bed in the middle of the night,
I'll not mind losing sleep and hold her very, very tight,
I'll tell her of a little girl who used to do the same,
Then sing our special song and cuddle her to sleep again.

Sinister

THE DECLINE AND FALL OF ADELE

By Jessie Hobson

PROLOGUE

London has many curious side streets for those who have time and inclination to explore. Some of them are home to unusual shops, especially those that collect and sell junk. Mostly the goods are just that, but now and again, some article of value may be found and enthusiasts will spend hours trawling through tat to find a bargain.

Mullin owned such a shop. He was approached one day by a dealer who supplied him with goods from abroad. He brought, among other things, a small grey statue which he claimed was of authentic Egyptian antiquity.

"Yeah?" said Mullin. "Sez you and whose army?" The dealer protested that the statue was genuine. Mullin looked it over and named a price. The dealer feigned shock and suggested double. In the end, they haggled to half-way between and Mullin added the grey figure to his stock. Some idiot with more money than sense would probably buy it if he plugged it as a real gem, he thought.

CHAPTER ONE

Adele's skin glowed, warm milk chocolate, surmounted by a tightly curled cap of black hair. To an onlooker, this would have emphasised the firm, smooth line of her jaw and the limpid black pools of come-hither eyes. But there was no-one there to see her beauty as she stepped from the shower and gracefully enfolded her body in a vast white towel.

Once dry, she dressed herself carefully and examined her reflection in a cheval mirror standing in the corner of the bedroom. It was as if the whole room had been designed to enhance her elegant and languid nonchalance of movement. Early morning sunlight fell on the creamy walls, casting shadows of the window frames across the silken sheets of the king-size bed and caught a sparkle in the eye of the statuette upholding a standard lamp beside the mirror. No ordinary lamp this, having a great globe in place of the usual shade, supported by the figure of Amun-Re, Egyptian God of the Sun.

The bright colours of the figurine were picked up by a number of other gods and goddesses adorning the room, as Adele had a passion for collecting representatives of the Egyptian pantheon. Very few of the pieces were genuine antiques, but that did not worry her. She had dressed herself in a close-fitting white dress and matching jacket. She wore scarlet high-heeled shoes and a colourful scarab brooch was pinned to the lapel of her jacket. She looked stunning and she knew it.

With a flourish, she moved to collect a scarlet clutch bag from the bedside table, checking its contents as she left the room.

Across the city, another smart penthouse was witness to the early activity of Adele's admirer, Laurence. Tall as he was, he could only meet her eye to eye when she wore high-heeled shoes, but where she was slight, he was broad-shouldered and would catch the attention of every woman in the room for his gladiatorial good looks.

He sleeked back his hair, changed his mind and let some strands fall darkly across his forehead. He brushed his hand over imaginary specks of dust on his beige blazer and tugged at the creases of his brown trousers to ensure they hung straight.

By nature, he was easy-going but was keen to impress Adele and was trying to match her effortless style as he prepared to leave for the rendezvous.

Laurence strode from the room along the passage to the lift and courteously waved a small woman forward to enter before him. He did not notice her arrival, nor did he give her more than a perfunctory glance as the lift bore them steadily down to ground level.

"Hello," said the woman quietly. "I'm your new neighbour. The second penthouse."

"Ah," replied Laurence, somewhat taken aback. "How do you do?"

The conventional response drew a smile to her face. She said "Fine, thank you. My name is Martha Verity, by the way."

"Ah," repeated Laurence. "Yes, well, my name is Laurence Scrivener. Pleased to meet you."

By this time, Laurence had taken stock of the bright brown eyes and shock of unruly red hair that surrounded her homely face. He was vaguely aware of the flurry of her full skirt and the brisk purposefulness of her walk as they left the lift. She waved goodbye and he lifted his hand uncertainly in reply, pausing to watch her disappear into the morning crowd heading for work. He dismissed this Martha person from his thoughts and went in search of a taxi. Adele did not like to be kept waiting.

CHAPTER TWO

The penthouse where Adele lived was discreetly built on the existing roof area of a large Victorian building. There was indeed a lift, ancient, with ironwork open to view as it descended but Adele chose to use the stairs. She daintily picked her way down the stone steps, her heels clacking and echoing in the stair vault.

Men always flocked to her, like bees round a honey-pot and she had no intention of appearing eager when meeting Laurence. It would not do for him to know the depths of desire which burned within her. So she took her time, emerging into the open air through the substantial doorway with an unhurried air, her head held high as she walked towards the main thoroughfare. She could have taken her car but parking was always a nightmare at the heart of the city and it was not far to her destination. She had persuaded Laurence to accompany her on a visit to the British Museum to feast her eyes on the Egyptian antiquities.

As she approached the entrance she noticed a group of tourists. They were milling around a bearded man in exotic robes who was clearly giving them instructions. The language he spoke was unfamiliar. Adele slowed to watch, partly out of curiosity but mainly because a quick glance around had shown her that Laurence had not arrived.

To her annoyance and embarrassment, she realised that the orator was eyeing her up and down as if she were a prize cow in a cattle market. She made to move on but he moved swiftly to bar her passage.

"Beautiful lady." He leered rather than smiled and Adele shuddered at the sight of broken teeth nestling in the depths of the beard.

"Beautiful lady," he repeated. "You please help my people here to find way in museum."

She stood mesmerised by the effrontery of the man, appalled and yet fascinated by a snake-like aura that surrounded him.

"Sorry, old chap. 'Beautiful lady' is due to have coffee with me right now. You will have to find another guide."

Adele turned gratefully to Laurence who had arrived so opportunely behind her. She missed the sudden flash of hatred that Laurence received from the bearded man's eyes. Laurence blinked and steered Adele away from the museum.

"Perhaps we should give it a miss today with the likes of him around," he said. It was said decisively, brooking no argument and Adele for once was ready to be over-ruled. The pair moved off, unaware of the smouldering eyes of the tour leader, who watched them go, tapping his hand on his thigh with frustration. With bad grace, he shepherded the group towards the museum and they disappeared from view.

CHAPTER THREE

"That man scared me," confided Adele to Laurence as they sat over their coffee. The cafe had been half empty. There was a scattering of people but only one group of three. Probably parents and son, thought Laurence idly before he responded to Adele.

"He was a bit weird. Not the sort to meet in a dark alley."

"The awful thing is, I felt I knew him from somewhere," said Adele thoughtfully. "Perhaps that is why he approached me."

Laurence pondered her remark in silence. Although he knew Adele was British born, her ethnic background was African and the tour guide had certainly looked middle-eastern.

The noisy scrape of chairs saved him from commenting as the family of three rose from their table. They were talking as they came past and the father politely asked Laurence and Adele whether they could advise on the route to the Tower of London.

Adele said, "Could we share a taxi to go there with these people, Laurence? It might be an idea for us to take a trip on the Thames from there."

"Yes, why not? Would that be acceptable to you and your family?" he asked the man. "Our treat," he added as he saw hesitation in their faces.

"That is most generous of you. We are on a limited budget, as it is not cheap to come all the way from Australia. I believe you Brits call it 'down under'?"

Laurence nodded. "That's settled then."

It was a bit of a squash in the taxi, but amongst the laughter they quickly found themselves at ease as a group. The Australian couple said they were usually called Sol and Izzy Goddard and their son was introduced as Ace, short for Horace. Adele and Laurence admitted that their names were not normally shortened, but Sol joked that they would soon put a stop to that and called them Del and Larry.

Arriving at the Tower of London, the family joined the queue and Adele and Laurence headed for the river. They had all arranged to meet up for the evening meal at the hotel where the Goddards were staying.

"Fresh air on the Thames. Much better than stuffy old museums," teased Laurence as they boarded the steamer.

"Glad you approve," said Adele primly. "That family is nice, but I could not, would not, go round that gory Tower with the ghosts and tales of dungeons and prisoners."

The pair wandered down into the saloon and chose a table near the wide windows. Laurence left Adele to find out whether the bar was open yet, and noticed a smartly uniformed crew member with bright red hair moving among the passengers. His thoughts returned to his encounter in the lift — what was her name? — Martha?

The bar was still closed, so Laurence strolled back to Adele.

"This morning, I found out that I have a neighbour in the other penthouse," he told Adele.

"Really? What is he like?" asked his disinterested lady.

"She, actually. Red hair, a bit scruffy, friendly."

A tiny worm of jealousy crept into Adele's mind. Laurence seemed to be overdoing the lack of attraction of this woman. Could he find her more interesting than he made out? Why had he bothered to talk about her? Aloud, she said, "It takes all sorts, perhaps she's an academic."

Laurence realised he had hit a nerve and lightly changed the subject. For the rest of the trip, he was attentive and Adele was reassured.

CHAPTER FOUR

There was still much of the day left when they disembarked and Adele urged Laurence to take her to hunt for antiques in obscure junk shops which she visited from time to time in her search for Egyptian artefacts.

Laurence, who was a freelance writer for a couple of art magazines, was quite agreeable to this, as he could poke about among the paintings while Adele examined statues, jewellery and other items of real or imagined antiquity.

Their two interests had been the cause of their meeting only a couple of weeks earlier at an auction of fine art goods. It seemed by chance that both went to the coffee stall for a break. Adele accidentally dropped some coins from her purse when paying, and Laurence gallantly retrieved them and returned them to her. Their eyes and hands met in instant attraction, and conversation flowed easily between them. Both made successful bids for items they wanted, and they left the auction together at the start of a new adventure of getting to know each other.

Adele, being of a passionate, intense nature, was somewhat piqued to find Laurence laid back and seemingly casual towards her, little knowing that he was taking time before showing his real feelings. So she had played it cool as well, and their relationship was still at a superficial level. She now risked slipping her arm through his as they walked down back alleys to the junk shop she had suggested, and a frisson of electricity passed between them.

They entered the gloomy, cluttered shop with narrow aisles which forced them to separate, so each went in search of items of interest. Laurence found a print of Matisse and was examining it when Adele gave a cry.

"Look, Laurence. A statue of Seth. He's the bad guy of the Egyptian Gods — he killed and cut up his brother Osiris and spread the parts all over the countryside, because he wanted to be the greatest."

Laurence weaved his way towards her, then took the grey figure from Adele's fingers and turned it over.

"Sounds grisly," he commented. "Do you think this is genuine?"

Suddenly, he burst out laughing.

"This looks like that courier bloke outside the British Museum. Ugly brute, wasn't he?"

Adele snatched the statue back. Her face was grave as she stared at the stern visage of the god. It did indeed resemble the man who had accosted her, and for some reason, she felt afraid. The feeling passed quickly, however, and she bargained keenly with the shopkeeper to purchase this new god to add to her collection.

The pair returned to the open air to hear Big Ben striking five o'clock.

"Time to sort ourselves out for our dinner date."

Laurence hailed a taxi and they returned to their respective homes to change, arranging for Laurence to return to collect Adele at seven.

Once back in her penthouse, Adele carefully unwrapped her purchase and placed it on the coffee table in the centre of the lounge. She gazed at the god, fascinated and strangely, fearfully reverential. She had never felt such influence from the other statues she had acquired, and was at a loss to explain her sensations. Mesmerised, she slipped to her knees and bowed to touch her forehead on the floor in obeisance. After a moment she rose and backed away from the statue, subservience in every line of her body. Lowering her head submissively, she turned and left the room to prepare herself for the evening in a confused daze. When Laurence rang the bell punctually at seven, she went to answer the door, carefully averting her eyes as she passed the squat figure on the table, looking with mute appeal for help at the statues of other gods and goddesses as she passed them. They stared back at her impassively, and she felt despair in her heart.

CHAPTER FIVE

It was a subdued Adele who accompanied Laurence to their meeting with Sol and Izzy, which puzzled Laurence as she had seemed happy and carefree earlier. Their hosts greeted them warmly, and the tense look on Adele's face melted as they gathered with young Ace in the anteroom for drinks before the meal. Laurence was aware of an air of strength emanating from the lad, in spite of his youth, and thought he would be useful in a scrap. His view was re-inforced when it was mentioned in conversation that Ace was a black belt at Karate.

"Sol was attacked once when Ace was younger," explained Izzy. "So as soon as he could, he decided to take up martial arts to protect his father."

Laurence had noticed earlier that Sol limped slightly, and nodded his understanding.

"Good to have such a supportive son," he said.

"Yes, indeed," answered Sol. "He will be a worthy man to take over the sheep farm we have in the outback." At this point, the party was summoned to the dining room and they filed dutifully to their places.

They were consulting among themselves which dishes and wines to order when there was a disturbance at the door. The noisy group entered all talking loudly, aggressively pushing their way to vacant tables across the room. They were followed by the tour guide who had accosted Adele outside the museum.

"Oh, no," whispered Adele. "Whatever is he doing here?"

Sol turned to look.

"You mean Dr Ashrak Rashid? He's an archaeologist or something like that. He and his rowdy bunch were on our plane, so the tour operator must have booked them in here, like us. Do you know him?"

Between them Laurence and Adele explained the earlier encounter. Izzy tutted, Sol said "disgraceful" and Ace looked daggers but said nothing.

"Don't let him spoil your evening, dear," said Izzy. "Let's eat our food."

During the meal, Sol mentioned that the lounge of the hotel had a tiny dance floor, and wondered if Laurence and Adele would care to adjourn there.

"The band is small, like the dance area, but it is a pleasant room," he announced.

"That would be splendid, wouldn't it, Adele?" replied Laurence formally.

Adele smiled and agreed.

They finished their meal before Rashid and his group, and walked across to the lounge. Laurence guided Adele on to the floor, and for the first time, took her in his arms.

'We're making progress', he thought.

Sol and Izzy watched indulgently as the lovers held each other close, murmuring privately. Ace asked a girl from another family to be his partner.

The dancers were unaware of a glowering figure lurking in the shadows of the hallway, staring fixedly at Adele and Laurence. It was Rashid. After a pause, he went quickly to the reception and arranged for a hire car to meet him at the entrance. To the driver's surprise, his client simply sat in the back of the limousine and told him to wait.

It was nearly an hour before a taxi arrived at the front of the hotel and Adele and Laurence emerged from the door, arms round each other. They clambered aboard, waving a cheerful goodbye to their hosts who had come out to see them off.

"Follow them," commanded Rashid curtly.

"You're the boss," muttered the driver as he drove off.

"Be sure to remember that," snapped Rashid.

The two vehicles pulled out into the evening traffic and came to Adele's dwelling where Rashid noted the address then told the driver to return to the hotel.

By the house Adele started to get out of the taxi. She turned to Laurence and held out her hand.

"Come," she said, the invitation clear in her eyes.

Laurence slid from his seat and with one arm around her waist, paid off the taxi. They went inside, and the creaking, clanking lift became for them a journey to the stars, entwined closely together.

Without a pause, they went in to the king-sized bed. Under the soft light of Amun-Re's globe as the god watched kindly over them, they were transported to paradise.

The little grey god on the coffee table bided his time.

CHAPTER SIX

The lovers returned to earth with a bump in the morning when they realised they each had work commitments that day. Laurence was due to take some papers for his principal magazine to be published, and Adele was expected at a photo-shoot promoting clothes for John Lewis.

Adele fetched orange juice from the fridge to take back to Laurence in bed. Pain like a whip-lash bit into her back. With a cry, she dropped the glass and turned to stare at the statue of Seth on the table. Laurence appeared in the bedroom doorway, and she fled to his arms, trembling with fear.

"You've only broken a glass, love," said Laurence. "Was it a valuable one?"

Adele made an effort to pull herself together.

"No, no," she stammered. "It gave me a fright, that's all."

"You go and get dressed and I'll fix us some coffee."

Later they left together to go to their appointments. Adele took her car as the photography was taking place out of town, and when she dropped Laurence, she said "I'll call you on the mobile later to make sure you have got back, then I can come and collect you again."

She smiled saucily at him and he kissed her before leaving the car.

Adele had parked a short distance from Laurence's apartment block and she watched him as he walked away. She went to start the motor but the engine did not engage and stuttered into silence. She smiled to herself, realising her mind was still with her lover. She glanced up, to see him nearing the front of his home. As he approached, a small ginger-haired woman emerged and greeted him animatedly. The worm of jealousy awoke and stirred in Adele's mind. Had she been waiting for him? She recalled the passion of the previous night and the worm slept again. She firmly addressed the matter of starting the car and the engine responded so that she was able to drive off as Laurence entered the building and the red-head walked swiftly away.

Because Adele was looking across the road, she did not notice a car parked on the nearside which drew into the traffic behind her. Rashid had not wasted time once back in the hotel the night before, but had arranged for a self-drive car, and before dawn he had come back to Adele's road, parking with a clear view of the building. Even so, he nearly missed her, as Adele and Laurence had gone out of the back of the block to a small mews where she garaged her car. It was only by chance that Rashid saw the couple drive out from the alley and turn into the mainstream traffic.

It is not unusual for cars to follow closely in London's streets, so it was not until Adele reached the suburbs that she noticed that a certain white car seemed to be keeping pace with her, neither dropping back nor trying to overtake. Her destination was Finchley, a studio in a side road, and she realised that the white car still continued in her wake. She turned into the area beside the studio and looked back towards the roadway in time to see Rashid glance in her direction as he drove past. She locked her car and sped into the entrance of the building. Once inside, she leaned against the wall, her breath heaving, her eyes wild with fear. The man must be stalking her.

The studio door banged noisily open and the photographer came out and greeted her.

"There you are, Adele. We thought you had got lost."

"No, I'm sorry, I had to make a detour to drop a friend. It took longer than I expected."

The excuse sounded lame, even to herself, but she was thankful that the distraction meant her fear had not been noticed.

Throughout the day, the modelling work took her mind off the presence of Rashid. She decided to call Laurence on the mobile before venturing outside the building, to see if he could meet her on the way home. He suggested King's Cross Station, as she could find a space to park, and he would wait in the refreshment room.

As Adele left the studio driveway, she saw her fears were justified. Rashid was waiting in his white car and he immediately fell in behind her. She decided to ignore him except for an occasional glance to see if she had shaken him off. Relentlessly, he followed.

Arriving at the station concourse, Adele hurried to the coffee bar, hoping desperately that Laurence would already be there. He did not fail her, and she ran to him.

"Laurence, I'm being trailed by that horrid Dr. Rashid. He was behind me in a white car all the way to Finchley, waited outside and then followed me back."

Laurence held her away from him and looked with consternation at her frightened face.

"You actually saw him?"

She nodded and they both turned to look about the station. There was no sign of him but the crowds milling around them provided plenty of cover.

"We'd better go back to my place, then," said Laurence grimly. "Where is your car?"

Adele led the way, urgently dragging Laurence by the arm. Still no sign of Rashid. They drove off into the evening rush-hour. Laurence glared at every white car that came near. They did not see Rashid who had hung back far enough behind to keep track of Adele's car but not to be seen following. In spite of the arrow-straight Euston Road, the traffic was unable to increase speed, and Adele gripped the steering wheel in nervous concentration as she drove. When at last she was able to leave the busy main road, she sought to twist and turn in back streets to elude her pursuer. Neither she not Laurence guessed that Rashid was now aware of their destination. He had driven by a direct route and was already in the underground car park below Laurence's apartment block, awaiting their arrival.

Believing they had succeeded in throwing the enemy off the scent, Laurence and Adele stepped from their car confidently and headed for the lift.

The roar of an engine revving and driving straight towards them alerted them to his presence, and Laurence flung Adele from the path of the speeding vehicle, but was hit himself and spun sprawling at Adele's feet. Rashid's car braked with a screech and he leapt out, intent on abducting his beautiful prize. As he moved towards her the lift door opened and Martha stepped out. Realising he had been seen, Rashid rushed back to his car and drove off in haste.

Laurence groaned and sat up clutching his head. Adele and Martha moved to help him, but he waved them aside.

"I'll be alright. Let's get up to my apartment."

The two women guided him into the lift, then Adele gave Martha assurances that Laurence would be fine, thank you and he said no, an ambulance was not necessary. Martha watched the lift door close, an anxious frown on her face, before she went on her way.

Once back in the penthouse, Laurence sank down into his elegant Chesterfield with a dazed look on his face. Adele went to make some strong hot coffee. On her return she was shocked to see that he had slumped sideways on the couch; clearly he had been more injured than they had thought. She felt for his pulse and her blood ran cold. Frantically, she lifted his eyelids to see a blank stare. She rummaged in her bag for a mirror and held it by his nose, but there was no sign of breath.

In agony of spirit, she cried "Oh, Laurence, no. Don't leave me, my darling. I've only just found you."

CHAPTER SEVEN

It was at this point that Adele began to slide into the madness that governed her future actions. The little grey god she had come to fear exerted his influence over her state of mind and drove her onward in a downward spiral of irrational behaviour. She embraced the dead body of her lover, but gave no thought to contacting either police or hospital. Her concern was to ensure the passage of her precious charge on a safe journey to the after-life. Her studies of the Egyptian gods had introduced her to the practice of embalming bodies for just this purpose, and she began to plan how she might achieve this for Laurence.

First, she knew she needed to return to her home and bring back statues of the gods involved in death rites. As a preliminary to preparation for burial, the body needed to be dried. Where could she do this? She searched the penthouse and discovered that Laurence had a sunken bath which doubled as a Jacuzzi. She could immerse him in brine — forty days, was it? — then perhaps she could trace a source of natron and resin.... She blanched at the thought of needing to cut his body open to remove internal organs. She would have to do it. Not yet. One step at a time. Get the statues, buy loads of cooking salt. Oh, and plenty of bandages to wrap the body. These at least she could get from a supermarket and drugstore.

So ran her thoughts as she paced the apartment.

The phone rang.

She made no move, and the answer phone kicked in.

"Hey, Larry, this is Ace. Pa and Ma would like to meet up with you and Del before we all go home. I'll drop by tonight to make arrangements. Hope you'll be there. See you."

The instrument fell silent. Adele looked bleakly at it. How many hours did she have? It was already six o'clock. Would Ace understand?

With full force the recollection of how all this had come about returned, coupled with an intense rage at the action of Rashid. The knowledge that she needed to outwit him to collect the items she required to safeguard her love made her think. Rashid must not stop her. Surely she would be safer in a taxi, not alone in her own car. Having phoned for one she went cautiously from the building and bade her taxi-driver wait for her during the excursions to the penthouse, the supermarket and the chemist. The journey was uneventful and she returned to Laurence's apartment laden with carrier bags and with a box containing certain of her statues. Against her will, she had felt compelled to bring the little statue of Seth. He had no part in death rites, but he still held her in thrall. She set him up on a shelf apart from the other gods and goddesses and was aware of a sense of triumph emanating from his ugly grey form.

"You are behind all this, My Lord Seth," she said with certainty. "You are indeed a jealous god."

Her maddened mind seemed to hear derisive laughter. She turned away, and for the first time, wept bitterly.

On her return to the apartment block, she had been observed by Martha, getting out of the taxi with her bundles, as Martha drove her car into the garage below. Laurence had been dismissive of her help, so she was reluctant to push in where she was not really wanted but she was puzzled by Adele's bags. She decided to mind her own business, and went to her own penthouse.

Adele, meantime, had recovered her composure and was setting about preparing Laurence's body.

CHAPTER EIGHT

Sol and Izzy were packing. It was soon time to return to Aussie, after an enjoyable time in good old London Town. They were leaving it to Ace to organise a final meeting with Larry and Del, but it looked possible it was not going to happen, as Ace reported back about the answer phone.

"What time you calling there?" asked Sol of his son.

"Say, half seven?"

"Give us a call and we can join you, wherever you say, if you find them."

"Right-oh," said Ace and left to do his own packing.

On cue, Ace arrived at Laurence's penthouse and rang the bell. A dishevelled and distraught Adele opened the door. Ace stared in amazement.

"Del? You OK?"

"I — I — it's Laurence." Her glance roved distractedly round the room. Clearly she was not under normal control.

"Can you help? I need to fix him so his head is out of the water. The Egyptians didn't submerge the head, just the body."

"What the blue juice are you talking about?" said Ace, steering Adele into the penthouse.

I'm trying to embalm him," answered Adele plaintively.

Ace took a deep breath. "You mean, he's dead? How come? Where is he?"

"In here." Adele led the way to the side of the bath where Laurence's naked body lay.

"Do the police know?"

Adele shook her head slowly. "They can't bring him back to me. Only the gods can."

"The authorities need to know what happened, Del. Do you know?"

"Oh, yes." Adele pointed to the shelf with the grey statue. "Seth did it."

Ace could see that there was blood on Laurence's head and he went to look at the little grey god. There did not seem to be blood on that — anyway, surely Adele hadn't killed Laurence. There must be some other explanation.

"I'll get the police." Ace went to the phone.

"No, please, Ace, they'll take him away," pleaded Adele. Ace put a sympathetic arm round her shoulders.

"It's got to be done, Del. Be brave."

Adele turned and flung herself across Laurence's body. She wailed in misery, endearments pouring from her broken heart, her mind descending deeper into unreason.

CHAPTER NINE

The commotion caused by the arrival of police and mortuary attendants brought Martha to her door. She was able to tell of her encounter in the underground garage, and that some driver sped off from the scene in a white car.

By this time, Adele was incoherent. The police could make no sense of her version of events. Ace could add little of value and he was finally allowed to leave to inform his parents of the situation. The police surgeon realised Adele was mentally unstable and arranged for her to be taken into care. She had insisted on taking the grey god with her, and it was felt best to indulge her in this.

Laurence's body was taken for autopsy and was examined by Dr. Andrew Beeston, head pathologist. He confirmed that the head injury was consistent with a blow from a heavy object, and agreed it was possibly a car, because of other bruises and damage to the victim's body.

Police followed up the lead given by Martha. As the car was hired, it was some time before they connected Dr. Ashrak Rashid with the incident. He had returned to Egypt with his entourage of archaeology students. It was some months before painstaking analysis of the facts led police to request his extradition.

During the period of investigation, Adele had not immediately been absolved from complicity in Laurence's death. She had been kept in care under medical supervision. The distressed girl had spent hours in supplication to the little grey god. It took long weeks of patient persuasion from a psychiatrist to wean her away from her devotion to Seth. She mourned the death of her lover, and in this she was inconsolable. She had reached rock bottom. Life had little meaning for her.

EPILOGUE

It is sunset on the Nile and the barren hills are resplendent with vast monuments trumpeting the glories of Pharaohs of long ago. The Karnak Temple is now quiet, empty, the fellahin and tourists gone; any guardians are settled till morning.

In the shadows between the massive columns, shapes might be seen in ghostly movement around a funerary slab on which lies a shrouded figure.

Anubis, the jackal-headed God of Embalming, is bent over the body. Nearby stands Osiris, God of the Dead, in golden robes and wearing the white Atef crown flanked by feathers and horns. His wife Isis is beside him, an ankh in her hand. Her magical powers had restored her husband in ancient times. Their son, falcon-headed Horus, is prowling anxiously behind them. He pauses now and then to speak to little Maat, the Goddess of Truth.

As night begins to fall, Amun-Re descends in the west in a final burst of sunlight, ready for his journey through the twelve hours of darkness in his royal night-bark, accompanied by Osiris as they combat evil demons in the underworld to emerge triumphant in a new dawn.

No mortals here, but all the faces would have been familiar to Adele and Laurence. One exception — Anubis removes his jackal mask to reveal the face of Andrew Beeston, the pathologist who had performed the autopsy on Laurence.

Osiris, better known as Sol to the lovers, raises a hand in benediction as Anubis begins to unwrap the body on the slab. Isis, or Izzy, moves forward to administer her powers to restore life to

45

Laurence. His passage through present-day life has been a penance for disobedience to his master, Pharaoh Amenemhat, when serving as his scribe. He was forbidden then to consort with the Nubian slave, Manethut, because she belonged to the temple of Seth. A temple priest called Paneb had slain him for his defiance.

As the shrouds fall away, the esoteric chant of the goddess takes effect and Kel, for such was Laurence's name as a scribe, rises from the slab and kneels before Isis.

"Divine Mother-Goddess, you are merciful beyond measure to me. But what of Manethut? As Adele she has been wrongly suspected of my murder, when all she did was to try to ensure my safe passage to you."

Maat, homely Martha, comes forward. "Kel, fear not. Truth will prevail and Rashid — Seth's priest Paneb — is already suspected of being the guilty one."

Horus sweeps off his falcon mask to reveal the smiling face of Ace.

"The time will come when you will be re-united with your beloved. She has shown her love for you. I have bargained with Seth to free her from bondage. Be patient, a mortal lifetime is but a second in the life of the Gods. Lord Amenemhat has forgiven you and bids you follow him to his abode among the stars, home of the Gods."

Total darkness falls over the great temple like a curtain closing a drama. Only the faint glitter of distant stars remains.

Far away, Adele takes a squat grey figurine and drops it in the waste bin. Let some other poor soul suffer his enslavement. Her first step has been taken toward recovery.

JOYRIDE

By Trish Gibbs-Leake

The pram in which I lie
Is old and grey
With wooden handles and big wheels,
The hood pulled up
And she is pushing me.

Along we go,
The squeaking of the springs
Keep time with
My kicking legs,
I gurgle at her.

She smiles
We gaze at each other
And I am still now,
Silent, as I watch her blue eyes darken,
Darken with love

Or something else....

The pram is going faster now
The bumps are jolts and bounces
That at first seem fun,
Her knuckles whiten
Against the dark wood handle

Sinister
But still she smiles
So everything's OK?
Faster still
But wait,
The smile is changing

I see teeth
A grin that makes me howl
The white-wide eyes
And wet gleam of her face float near,
Screaming in my ears
Then one last push
And she lets go.

ONE OF OUR TRAINS IS MISSING

By David Shaer

"The train at platform four is your semi-fast twenty one hundred hours service to Shoeburyness via Basildon calling at...."

Everything else faded into the noisy background as it always seemed to after a long, weary, dreary day in the City of London dodging work and bombs. Sounds, sights and smells drifted into each other.

Although I had often floated away on auto-pilot at this time of night, the out-of-body experience never ceased to intrigue me. Part of me appeared to take a step backwards and upwards whilst another part seemed to fade into day-dream mode. I suppose that after twelve or thirteen hours at the coal face, one has to power down or lose one's sanity.

It was already becoming dark as, in this automatic mode, I glided through the first door of the fourth carriage — always the same door for more than twenty years, although I could never work out or remember why — I chose my normal first option seat in a bay of four, by the aisle, facing the back of the train....what weird creatures of habit we humans really are! Absolutely no logic other than possibly more space, albeit countered by the chance that the remaining three seats might be taken later by supporters of either an East London football team or members of a neo-fascist political party boarding at Barking. Much more likely, however, would be a pirate like boarding by a couple of invertebrate, inebriate 'suits' falling out of an hostelry in Fenchurch Street.

Tonight the fates, or so I thought, smiled sweetly upon me and the distance of the fourth carriage from the ticket barrier proved sufficient to deter any late arrivals.

I spread my few belongings — a suit jacket on the overhead rack, a briefcase on the empty window seat next to me — and slipped into those first few moments of euphoria. The train crept slowly forward, albeit backwards to me, and I sank into a warm, soporific glow. The increasing speed eluded me as I floated gently away into that peaceful phase between life and unconsciousness.

We sailed further away from the last vestiges of the setting sun into the rapidly blackening night of oblivion, when suddenly I heard for the first time a sad, limp whistle from the past. The sound was immediately swallowed by the modern whine of the c2c electric 357 unit which, in turn, was countered by the deep, thrusting roar of the hissing, heavy champing blast of something enormous and unbeknown to most — the fully pressurised, powerful thunder of an old fashioned, fiery steam engine. The screaming hiss of the pistons, the clanking of driving rods, the barking cough of the exhaust, everything that culminated in the sound of power and drive of a wonderful state-of-the-ark steam driven Stanier 3 cylinder 2-6-4 tank engine originating from the 1930s. It was obviously under pressure and hauling a heavy load.

All around me, people drifted in and out of slumber but nobody seemed interested — except for the rather mature chap immediately opposite me. He was smartly attired but not of this era. He was wearing a hand made three piece pin-striped suit with a handkerchief peeping out from his breast pocket. His shirt was good quality silk and his grey silk tie was too narrow. Not many of us still have shiny black laced up brogues on after dark but, besides these, he sported a pocket watch with a gold chain. Come to think of it, I didn't even remember the arrival of this old chap opposite me but then I had floated in and out of sleep since we left the terminal.

The sound of the approaching steam train was not normal. We were obviously overhauling it from behind and still very few of my fellow passengers seemed interested. This was a power that seemed to be unknown to most of these modern-day young passengers. Still only I and the mature traveller opposite seemed to notice. The vibrations of strength and pure power could be felt through the flimsy structure of each of the modern carriages. The whole trembling of the electric train left it feeling vulnerable, flimsy, paper-thin and thoroughly exposed. Slowly we began to overtake the dark, maroon, smoky and filthy old carriages of the steam train, each dimly lit but visibly full, very full, of upright, seated and strangely lifeless passengers — rigid and well dressed, as though they had been attending a serious function. As we approached the front of the train, the hiss of the pounding pistons grew louder and stronger until, finally, there it was — the heading tank engine, puffing, screaming and crying its way forward in full steam. The engine was disgustingly dirty, faded and rusty. But powerful. Oh such strength. The scraping of corroded tracks, the squeaking phlanges, the screeching of oxidised metal against other oxidised metal scraping like fingernails against a blackboard.

The hairs on the back of my neck rose to attention. Crude pimples leapt upward on my forearms. My teeth grated and the blood ran chilled through my veins. I shivered with cold as something or someone passed through me. The emotions of both admiration and fear coursed beyond control through my body. And still, no-one else seemed to take any notice, except the man with the pocket watch and the gold chain.

We both stared transfixed out of the window not wishing to miss a moment of this strange event. For a moment I glanced at him. His attention, however, was totally devoted to the power and thrust of the steam engine. As I turned my attention back, our train began to brake and the steam train started to accelerate past us, first the engine, then an empty guard's van followed by the single Ladies Only compartment in the first carriage — a feature that had long since disappeared from the facilities offered. The compartment was full — about twelve ladies each of whom was prim, well presented and fully engrossed. One, in particular, caught my eye. She appeared tall, seated as she was, with a silk, high necked, starchy white blouse, white lace gloves that extended up her wrists and a wide, tight brown leather belt that seemed to cut into her shapely small waist. She wore a light coloured bonnet that was tied neatly under her chin, which was delicate, and silky, just like the skin of her face, the only skin visible. On her lap was a small bag from which she took a small white cotton handkerchief and dabbed at her nose, a small upturned feature that gave her an impression of sweetness, innocence and intrigue. She then

51

used the handkerchief to touch, with complete delicacy, the corners of her mouth which was beautifully shaped, petite and implied that she was not a working girl. In fact, she looked to belong to a different era altogether and appeared out of place amongst the others around her. They all seemed to come from the fifties like Mr. Goldchain. Alas, the moment passed too quickly as the old steam train continued to accelerate away and the figures within the other compartments merged into each other as they flashed by into the night.

As suddenly as it had appeared, the old train vanished and I turned back to my fellow passengers to see if anybody else had shared my moment. Sadly the man with the golden chain and pocket watch had gone, for it was he to whom I felt I could talk, if only to confirm that I had not been dreaming. But there was an empty seat where he had originally been. Perhaps he had disappeared to stretch his legs.

My train had now slowed to a crawl and outside, on both sides, was only a collection of sad and empty dilapidated old warehouse buildings. It seemed that we had gone back in time to the era of the earlier steam train. There were no lights anywhere and the only aid to looking at the warehouses came from the lighting within our train. Gently we came to rest, as though the power had vanished since there was no sound of braking. We sat in silence, broken only by the odd voice further down the carriage, where conversation was limited to the toneless meanderings of an over-indulger whose contribution was restricted to the constant repeating of vulgarity occasioned by his mind's inability to command the more complicated rudiments of his mother tongue. It is amazing how coarse and crude the words falling from the mouth of an ill-educated drunk can seem to fellow travellers when they have nowhere to hide.

One minute lapsed into other minutes and the sound of silence became total as the distant drunk passed into a coma. Not even the electrics of the train gave out a hum and I was unsurprised when the lights started slowly to grow dim. Nowadays there is always a comedian present full of useless banter such as "Anybody got a match or am I going blind? 'Ow many fingers 'ave I got up, Sharon?" — inevitably followed immediately by a series of quick fire Essex girl quips. But after about five minutes, even these dried up and silence was restored. The lights faded further and it became apparent that nothing was working — normal lights, emergency lighting, doors, speaker systems and ultimately the heating. Outside the empty warehouses began to take on much clearer images and more passengers began to strain their eyes into the empty gloom. When finally all of the train's interior glowing lights had faded completely and total darkness reigned, then the first stages of a passenger uprising and revolution started to be heard. Within minutes, some of the more adventurous began to organise working parties intent on breaking out, although nobody had yet devised a method. None of the emergency door opening routines seemed to be functioning and the air was becoming rancid.

Somebody inconsiderately decided to light a cigarette and was almost instantaneously mugged by a surrounding group of apparent asthma sufferers. Another passenger advised anybody who was listening that he was going to smash a window to let some air in but was dissuaded on the basis that the only available tool was a special security device for that very purpose but it had already been vandalised and could not be found in the dark. The comedian offered his wife's tongue in its place but since she was obviously not the giggling girl seated next to him holding his hand, she was an unavailable substitute. Not a single mobile telephone could pick up a signal, so it rapidly became obvious that we were there for a long wait, although no-one could actually be sure where 'there' was. Normally I was one of those sad 'anoraks' who could tell exactly where he was by listening to the track as we moved, knowing all the curves, points, speed restrictions and tunnels or bridges as we passed them. Since, however, I had been distracted by earlier events, I could not help and I certainly had no idea from where the warehouses had sprung. I was totally lost.

However, I thought I could hear in the distance a faint whistle and I felt sure that the sound of the panting of steam engine pistons was coming back again. But once again, I seemed to be on my own. Although people had started to talk, an unheard of event except in times of crisis, nobody seemed to have heard the sounds that I felt sure were approaching. A further whistle followed by the sound of screeching brakes floated in and yet still no-one seemed to react. Nobody was paying attention as, with a vicious, metal rending jolt, our train suddenly leaped backwards as if something had crashed into the front of it. A single scream echoed throughout the carriage, repeated almost instantly as a second smashing jolt hit us. But this time the movement of the train continued and we started to roll backwards in the direction from which we had come. It was as though the old steam train had come back to rescue us but still I appeared to be the only one who could sense it.

Our backwards movement continued in little jolts, larger each time until gradually they became smoother and we began to gather speed, still, however, in darkness and stilted silence. Suddenly, with a triumphant peep of its whistle, and just as quickly as it started, the steam train gave one final shove and seemed to fade away back into the distance. Our reversing roll was to me now totally uncontrolled as we began to career faster and faster, obviously down an increasing gradient. An uncomfortable rocking motion started to set in and the speed began to worry me. Not apparently so the other passengers, though, who just seemed to be happy that we were on the move again, albeit still in total darkness and backwards.

My paranoia began to switch from worry to fear, as I thought of the implication of a backwards rolling runaway. It was obviously not going to stop until it ran into something, probably an approaching high speed train travelling unaware of the unlit mass hurtling towards it the wrong way up the down track. I stood and struggled my way through the darkness towards the doors hoping that I might be able to hit the emergency alarm which, in theory, should trigger the emergency brake. I knew, however, that without power, the train should not be moving. All brakes should have automatically come on, in the same way that it should not be possible to drop a lift since the emergency brakes, the wall guides in the lift shaft, should always come together to catch the falling lift. Since some of the very first train crashes, the safety devices had always meant that any failure of power or hydraulics would immediately throw on the brakes even if, or especially if, a brake pipe had broken. So why were we hurtling backwards out of control?

As I made it to the nearest doors, I ran my hand up the doorpost to the emergency button and almost broke all of my fingers as I stabbed it with more force than I realised I possessed. Nothing — apart from the excruciating pain of damaging my fingers. It was always possible that even in an emergency, a message would be issued to a disinterested signalman thirty miles away warning him to radio the driver and ask him to ascertain "which idiot had leant against the emergency button causing the train to pull up smoothly at the next station". The train, however, continued to accelerate and the speed was now beginning to produce a seriously uncomfortable ride, which, for trains capable of 100 m.p.h., was even more worrying. I retreated to my seat, barking my shins on all sorts of unknown, unseen but solid objects.

My fear had now progressed beyond the terrifying paranoia, yet still no-one else seemed concerned. Where was my man with the gold chain and pocket watch? He would support me on this, I felt sure. But before I could trace him with a blinding flash the train hurtled through a brightly lit station — so fast that I could not read any of the signs as they flew past the window. Just as we roared back into darkness, I glimpsed, or thought I glimpsed, a name. Maryland. Where the hell was Maryland?

Still our speed increased and the rocking motion had now degenerated into a snatching sideways roll as well, heading rapidly towards the inevitable moment when the train would either begin to disintegrate or simply lurch onto its side. People around me began to appreciate the dilemma and the tension was mounting. Passengers were beginning to cling to each other and were moving rapidly into seats so that they were travelling backwards to absorb to force of the impending disaster. The downhill motion became worse and my jacket flew off the rack, accompanied by several other, but much heavier articles. Bags, coats and umbrellas began to fly around and passengers started to scream. This did not bode well, particularly since the coaches were still in virtually total darkness.

With an ear-splitting bang, the suspension of the carriage collapsed to one side and, in almost slow motion, the whole carriage started a determined list that seemed destined to end in a roll. The track underneath us was now screeching and the sound of flying gravel began to rattle like machine gun fire against the underside of the bodywork. The track curved away in the same direction as the list of the carriage like a vicious fairground roller coaster where G-forces become absorbed in a corkscrew-like motion. With a sickening shudder the leading end of the carriage leapt into the air and the motion of the whole train began a slow, twisting spirally upwards, not unlike the fuselage of a jet fighter launching into a steep victory-rolling climb.

Instantly the clattering, crunching, banging and scraping ceased and, apart from the moaning and sobbing of the passengers, an eerie silence prevailed, the only other sound being the whistle of the wind passing rapidly through the framework of the train. We seemed to be flying, albeit still in a slow corkscrew motion. Both outside and inside all was dark as we continued to climb. Time appeared to freeze and soon we just seemed to hang but still spiralling slowly. As the carriages began to level and the rate of climb eased off, we hung suspended as in a slow flying tube, not dissimilar to an aircraft fuselage. Outside, images began to appear, mostly filtered through a gentle yellow to amber glow, like sodium street lighting. In fact, that was exactly what we could see, through a dim haze. The ground below, rows of lights, gradually became visible. These were obviously street lights and the spiralling slowed down further until we began to adopt the attitude of a level flying glider. Still the wind whistled around us but everything became calm and smooth and we seemed to be floating as if on a magic carpet.

To all intents and purposes, it looked as though we were following a straight line of sodium lights, almost in the way that old fashioned aviators followed roads, rivers or even railway lines. There seemed to be a logical progression in our journey and we even began to bank slowly, first left, then right, as though we were in a gliding space shuttle making a long planned approach after re-entry into the earth's atmosphere. Except there was no atmosphere, there were still no interior lights — only the whistle of a glider floating through the air. Soon, however, the sound began to change and a gentle hiss started to slide into the whistle, like the sound of a leaking pressure cooker. The attitude of the train started to change, as though it really was an aircraft turning from downwind and beginning its final approach. Almost expecting to hear flaps extending and undercarriage lowering into a locked position, I somehow began to feel as though this was planned and whatever was going to happen next would almost be logical. The hissing grew even louder and was beginning to sound exactly like a leaking brake pipe on an old steam train.

The stark realisation of what was happening suddenly hit me. We were, in fact, trying to 'come in to land', albeit inside about 240 tons of ill-designed equipment that was totally inadequate as a flying machine. We were about to encounter the worst ever planned heavy landing, without a runway, an aircraft or even a level playing field. Never mind assuming a crash position, this was going to be, in insurance terms, a total. Taking one's spectacles off would be about as much use as a collapsible umbrella in a tornado. The hissing grew louder still and I swear that I could even hear the beating of pistons from the old steam engine.

My heart, which I assumed had stopped beating long before, suddenly started to bang and crash around inside my chest and I could almost feel the bruising beginning to show. My stomach announced its presence by churning upside down and I just knew that I was going to be sick. This really was going to be a proper coming down to earth with a bang and nothing was going to help any of us. We were starting to gain momentum and we were beginning our descent. Below the train, I could begin to make out a familiar sight, the burn off flares of the refinery at Corringham. We were coming back into land on the marshes near Pitsea, in fact immediately over the railway track from Stanford. There really was no hope as we started to sink gently, in almost a perfect approach routine. At least we would come down on marshland, although what I thought that would do to make anything easier, I really don't know.

The approach was not as expected, however, because I could see Basildon almost below us and we were beginning a slow right bank as we seemed to line up over the cuttings approaching Vange. Oh how the ancient aviators would have been impressed. The right bank was insufficient because we were now roaring down towards Pitsea Station and that lies on a vicious left curve which the train seemed to be straining to lean into. Further and further over to the left the train began to lean, still sinking. We seemed to be in trouble and the left list was getting worse. Through the window looking directly below us, I could see that we were now only feet from the ground, straight above the track. With a horrible, sickening screaming of metal against metal, we began to run into the track and sparks started to fly. This was it — we really were crashing. The sound of shattering glass, the ripping of metal, the screaming of real people suddenly broke through the violent hissing and we started what was obviously going to be a disintegration process like that ill-fated burn up upon re-entry. Somehow, I could hear the accompaniment of a steam train's screaming whistle as the hissing grew even louder and the ripping apart of the train started. A belly flop on an aircraft would be a terrifying and expensive process but this was destined to be much more terminal.

Momentarily the train seemed to hold it together and although we were definitely now sliding out of control on our side, we seemed to be intact. Still we were hurtling along the track with sparks flying, glass being sprayed everywhere and metal panels being ripped away from their rivets. Was I mistaken? It seemed as though we were actually beginning to slow down and the train was still predominantly complete. After what seemed an eternity, the sliding, crashing, sparking mass of metal and glass was actually coming to a halt and it seemed as though it wasn't about to self destruct after all. I was in a train crash but it really looked as though I was going to survive, as were most, if not all of the people around me. And there he was — the man with the pocket watch and gold chain — I'm sure he winked. And then, just as suddenly, he wasn't. But we had actually come to rest.

Trying to open a door was not a problem. There were no windows left anywhere so climbing up and out was easy. Anyway the door was easy to push up and it banged back on its hinges onto the outside of the carriage. I could hear doors all along the train banging open and people were beginning to climb up and out. People were laughing, crying, clapping, almost singing; those who had survived. But still I could hear the hiss of escaping steam. Something wasn't right. As I climbed out through the door, I stood up on the side of the carriage and realised that it was dirty, maroon and made of wood. The hiss grew even louder and towards the front of the train, I could see a red glow and people running around. I wasn't on the electric train. This was the old steam train and the glow was the engine also lying on its side with the firebox ripped open. In fact I could now see that the engine was at the far end of the Benfleet Station platform and was tangled up with something that looked like a car.

Curiosity forced me to advance further along the carriage until I could see that the tangle also included buckled, twisted and severed level crossing gates. We had run into a car, an old Standard Vanguard, on the level crossing at Benfleet. There wasn't a great deal of the car left and the steam engine on its side seemed to be gasping its last breath. One of the four crossing gates was still standing but another was buried in the side of the signal box and I could see the signalman inside running around ringing bells and hauling back levers. He was obviously trying to warn off any other approaching trains and throwing signals to red.

It suddenly dawned on me that, after all my years of travelling, I had been involved in my first train crash but it was one that had happened on a dark night in March 1955, more than fifty years ago. I had survived and was probably going to be just a 'column-inch statistic' in the News Chronicle. As I began to realise the implications, I could feel my legs beginning to buckle. Somehow, I clambered down onto the platform and just sank to my knees. This was a real out of body experience and all I could do was sit down and rock backwards and forwards trying to breathe and grasp the seriousness of what was happening. I began to realise that there were people in the carriages lying on their sides next to me but all I could do was rock backwards and forwards and shake. I was powerless and useless.

"Cup of tea, sir?" asked a well spoken but kindly voice. I strained to raise my head and found myself being stared at by the beautiful young lady I had seen earlier, sitting on the old steam train. She stood there, still wearing her silk, high collared blouse, her lace gloves, her bonnet. Her skin was as silky as I remembered it, her waist still tightly sealed by her belt. She was wearing a simple, grey pleated skirt that came almost down to the ground, where she was presented in neatly laced small black ankle boots, straight out the Victorian era and so out of place.

"Sir?" she repeated and again I had to force my head upwards. She was standing behind a small, makeshift trestle table that was covered by a neatly ironed plain white table cloth on which stood a bone china cup and saucer, a small teapot and a delicate white milk jug. She had to be a dream. I was rendered speechless and the young lady perceived this instantly.

"Look, Sir, I shall pour you a strong cup but I am going to put some sugar in it — you are probably in a state of shock. Just stay there and I'll bring it to you".

Staying there, as she put it, was easy. It was about all I could do. With that sweet smile and her demure and steady hand, she poured tea as though it was the most beautiful movement created, added a splash of milk, then conjured up a bone china sugar bowl from which she scooped several teaspoons full of sugar and, with natural flair, stirred the cup's contents with amazing dexterity as though her very life had been created just for that sole purpose. I sat mesmerised as, with totally steady gloved hand, she raised the cup and saucer and almost floated round the table towards me. As she approached, I froze, open mouthed, speechless. She took just two light paces towards me and started to stoop over. As she held the tea in front of me, I gazed with awe into her eyes — beautiful light grey, crystal clear eyes, as clear as her soft skin — a total vision of beauty whose very presence rendered me powerless. I could see she was holding out the cup and saucer but I was completely incapable of raising a hand to take it. She started to kneel next to me and brought the cup to my lips. She was now so close that I could smell her perfume, her very breath and still I sat transfixed. She placed her gloved hand to the back of my head and began to tilt the cup to my mouth. It is not possible to describe the experience of the taste of nectar but at that moment I was rendered incapable of anything. It was an unparalleled experience that the power of speech would have impeded. I took a sip of the sweet liquid and could feel myself floating. Nothing in this world had I ever tasted was as perfect — this was my moment of total euphoria.

"Just lie there for a moment, Sir," the voice seemed to come at me from far away. "I'll see if I can find a blanket. Don't worry, I'll fetch you another tea and we'll get someone to help you in a minute."

"Don't go, please," I begged "I don't even know who you are."

"Oh, it doesn't matter," she breathed.

"Well it does to me," I responded, slightly too quickly but tact is not one of my personality traits. She was standing up and I could feel her moving away from me and I didn't like it. I just wanted her to stay with me until I could gather my thoughts.

"Look," she whispered, "my name is Amelia Elizabeth — Beth to my family"

"What is it to your friends?" I bludgeoned forth and she turned and smiled. Oh, what a smile. I remembered the lips she had dabbled earlier but now I could see the dimples in her cheeks as she smiled and her teeth — so white, so shiny and so perfectly small and delicate.

"Milly, Sir, with a 'Y'" and she turned back and carried on walking away. I felt myself sinking back into oblivion. This was going to be a moment I intended to remember, whatever the outcome.

I could hear vague, soft sounds around me and a harsh light began to penetrate my eyes. Perhaps I wasn't dead after all. Perhaps I was. The brightness and the noise began to filter through.

"Come on, sir, wake up, you're going to be fine". I lay there needing much more convincing than that. I hurt. My head, my arms, my legs — everything really hurt.

"Here, try to drink a sip of water — but no throwing up this time, please". Now I definitely wanted to stay asleep. The voice was soothing and in control.

"Look, sir, you've been in an accident but you're alright. You're in hospital but not to worry. We'll have you up and about in no time at all. They can do miracles with modern science now". It went dark again.

"Where the hell have you been?" a voice yelled. It was angry, I could tell. It wasn't just the fact that the owner was leaning out of his office door in my direction with venom oozing from his pores, it was the swollen eyes bursting to get out of their sockets. Something had obviously upset his equilibrium and I had a feeling that I may have had something to do with it.

"Two bloody days you've been missing and not so much as a bloody phone call. Don't you realise that everybody has been up to their necks in crap for a month and all you do is just disa-bloody-ppear without a single word. If we weren't so bloody stretched, you'd be down the bloody road now! Where the fu…. nah! I don't wanna know. Just get your arse in here — now."

What had happened? How did I get here? What happened to Milly? To hospital? To modern science? I still felt bruised and hurt. I was struggling to remember anything, including my very name.

Before he started up again, I shuffled my way forward looking around me for support but it was blatantly obvious that this guy wasn't the only person who was less than happy with me. Something unpleasant had surely happened but I was completely oblivious of whatever it was. I assumed the vulgar man was my Boss and it was only as I entered his office, automatically shutting the door behind me, did I notice that his wall calendar was covered in red ink, looking as though it had been slapped on with rage during a fit of pique. All was not well — sometimes I can be quite perceptive, really. It was the "two days missing" bit that was giving me a problem. As far as I was concerned, I had left work last night and come back in this morning.

Apart from a Milly and a hospital, both of which still confused me, I thought that I was just a little late for work and slightly forgetful. Names obviously come back quickly.

It seemed, however, that I was misreading the situation quite badly here because, as I took an unoffered seat in front of him, the Boss opened a drawer and took out what appeared to be my personnel file. As he slammed it onto his desk, I thought that I might have been here before. This was a man with an attitude which was vaguely familiar. And it wasn't bringing back good memories. A plethora of little yellow 'Post-it' notes were attached down the side of sheets within the file and I began to feel a distinct sense of uneasiness. It wasn't helped by the Boss's opening a large exercise book and tearing out a blank sheet of paper and engraving my name with venom on the first line. Maybe I didn't want this job after all.

It probably would not have been smart at this point to pass into 'out of body' mode but the temptation was indeed very great. The pages indexed with yellow 'Post-it' markers were flicked open and a rapid list of notes entered on the blank sheet. In view of the earlier veiled threat, this was obviously a 'yellow card' affair rather than a full 'red card' but even I sensed that it would not be prudent to be anything other than humble. As he drew to a close, the Boss was becoming edgy and I had a feeling that he had been put up to this. He seemed to be the sort of person who would have issued a metaphorical 'knee in the groin' statement allowing me to re-iterate my humble apologies and then we would probably have gone over the road for a beer and he would have given me an unofficial 'good kicking'. But this was different. He was embarrassed. This was going to be official and was going to hurt.

Unauthorised absence? Good God, Man — I'm sure that we had often stayed over the pub for more than an hour at lunch time and on more than one occasion, we had ended up so 'legless' that diplomacy required that we just slipped away and got somebody else to turn off our computers feigning that we had a meeting 'out of the office' all afternoon. Yes — it was coming back to me.

But two whole days. What? What on earth was he talking about?

Of course I had been in. I had never played truant unless it was with him. Things did not add up. Yesterday had been a normal day and I had left about 8:00pm and caught the 9:00pm train. OK, I had had a couple rather than go straight home but that was purely because I had been in for nearly twelve hours without a break and I would have killed someone if I had just run for the 8:00pm train. I could even remember what I had been working on — it was the consolidated forecasts for October to December and the start of the next year's budgets. As far as I was now concerned, I remembered that he should have known this because I had sat with him a week earlier to discuss the principles behind the revised forecasts for the rest of the year and, in his absence on a trip, I also remembered that I had been through the Managing Director's Department costs directly with the MD, including his vastly excessive salary and bonus provisions. Perhaps I had said that rather than just thought it.

But that was two whole days ago, not yesterday apparently and I started to doubt my sanity. Upon standing up and banging my Boss's desk, I got the feeling that I was burying myself alive. But, as usual, I fired from the hip and duly shot myself comprehensively in the foot. "Well since it's only Tuesday today...."

"Thursday."

"....and tomorrow is Wednesday, I...."

"Friday,"

".... oh, Boy — what's going on here?"

"You tell me."

I sat down deflated and tried to cast my mind back. But nothing would come. I could remember absolutely nothing about either Tuesday or Wednesday.

"I think perhaps I should go back to bed and start all over again," slipped out.

"Actually, if you walk out of here right now, you can keep going," came the witty retort. I got the very distinct impression that he meant business, so I capitulated and started my grovel of humiliation — not that I really knew how to do that. But, since jobs do not grow on trees, tact, diplomacy and sacrifice seemed to be a sensible step forward.

"Apart from the MD's section, because he has reserved the right to change his figures should he so desire — his words not mine," I squirmed, "the forecasting will be finished today and I should have finished next year's budget by tomorrow night," "Bloody right," the reply came, "in fact you should have finished it last bloody week." Oh how I knew I was on a loser, adding quickly "I can give you rough drafts now, if that helps, but they will be very rough and very draft." Oops. Bad move.

"Well if they're that bloody rough, I don't want to waste my bloody time on them at all." I began to realise that staying silent was the only thing likely to help me. "And if you do deign to come in tomorrow, for Chrissake put some clean clothes on and shave. You were wearing that smelly old crap on Tuesday and you're not growing a bloody beard in here." Would that Scotty were still around to beam me up. I struggled to stand without being noticed and slide out backwards and below radar level before the next barrage was released.

"And don't think that grovelling for the next 24 hours is going to get you out of this shit. You're gonna have to do shed loads of brown nosing to turn this one round, you stupid bastard and not just to me." I think I was getting the picture — very loud and very clear.

So by the time I had slunk away with my tail well and truly drooping between my legs, the prospect of going home early to catch up on sleep appeared not to be an option. In fact even going out for lunch was not really worth considering either. The main object was to produce my earlier expected figures and just hope that nobody would even attempt to read them until they had been proven. The metaphorical prevailing wind was head on and relentless and the storm did not look like subsiding in the foreseeable future.

The day seemed to cling overhead and refused to come to my rescue. Every corner I turned seemed to have a man carrying a plank coming the other way but today some of the planks also had large rusty nails hanging out of them. Everything dragged on for ever and it was no surprise when I suddenly realised that many of my colleagues had already drifted off home and I was only just starting on the budgets. This was going to be a long night. By seven o'clock the office heating had turned itself off and I could feel the cold creeping into the very marrow of my bones.

By eight, I was having trouble staying awake at all and decided that a tactical retreat was called for, with an ultra-early start the following morning. I slipped silently away down the back fire exit and headed off towards Fenchurch Street accompanied by my low esteem. Friday was going to be very hard but at least I might have an idea about what was going on, whereas today had been totally beyond my comprehension.

As I dragged my forlorn body up the predictably non-functioning escalator at the station, my mind somehow wandered back to a pretty girl with a silky face and a high-necked sparkling white blouse. The sensation was more intrigue rather than lust because the cumulative effect of the week to date had already rendered my body as a wasted cause. Walking up a stationary escalator is always much harder than anyone realises but the effect this night was tantamount to a first stage coronary with pain in my shoulders, my legs and even my jaws. The oxygen just wasn't making it. However, her image still kept coming to me — her pale skin, her perfectly shaped waist, her smiling dimples but, most of all, her sweet breath. I could almost feel the delicate touch of her hand on the back of my head. She was definitely real and my mind was racing with thoughts, unanswered questions and confusion. From where had she come?

The 20:30 was my next train but I was going to have to leap up the last five or six steps to respond to the sound of a guard's whistle on the concourse indicating the train's imminent departure. This just wasn't my lucky day and I had already given up hope as I surfaced onto the upper level. The orange lights on the train's doors were still showing but I was too far away to be able to scramble through the ticket barrier, not that I could find my season ticket anyway. As I made my last effort, there, about 50 metres ahead, she stood — my vision of beauty, with her dainty lace-gloved hand almost pressing on the door button. Before I could think, she had opened the doors, disappeared and the doors had closed behind her, extinguishing their orange indicator light. The train started to move and my day drew to a sad and dismal close. I had probably made her up.

Aimlessly, I meandered over to the 20:40 all stations crawling train.

As I sank into my seat, it was amazing how things mysteriously started to come back to me. At first I could remember sounds, weird old alien ones and a feeling of fear began to invade me. The nervous sweat of paranoia was trickling through my veins and goose pimples crept all over me. I felt sure that people around me could see that my hair was standing on end and a sensation of panic was beginning to take over my head. Something weird was happening over which I had absolutely no control and I didn't like it. I felt sure that my left eye was beginning to twitch and that everybody was staring at it. Conversation around me stopped instantly and people started to whisper behind diversionary protective hands. Short of breaking into conversation and asking what they were thinking or talking about, I deemed it to be a better part of valour to move into yet another part of the train and forget what was happening here. The train had now left and I was just very pleased to be going home.

With an unrelenting certainty, I was sure that I was definitely losing it. The stress of whatever had happened was all too much and I was starting to fall apart. I sat down again and sought to hide behind a screen of slumber. Drifting off was instant. The floating sensation took over.

"Hey, are you alright, mate?" a deep voice enquired from somewhere. My eyes were shut and I wanted them to stay that way. Please go away. "Hey, Sunbeam, do you need a drink of water or summat? You look like shit!" Actually, I felt like shit but telling me wasn't going to make it any better. The voice, however, was obviously not going to go away and with great reluctance I slowly forced open one eye. There, in front of me, staring straight into my sore eye was a strange old chap with a scruffy grey pinstriped suit, a dark grey shirt and matching tie with a worn, stiff and slightly grubby white collar and, something which caught my eye immediately, a pocket watch with a gold chain. He resembled, at first glance, a funeral director, despite the fact that I didn't have a clue what a funeral director looked like.

The gold watch confused me. I got the distinct feeling that I had seen it before. But before I could plough back into the recesses of my jaded mind, he lunged forward towards me, brandishing a plastic bottle partly filled with water. I don't normally accept used bottles from strangers but I had a need and he certainly seemed a tad insistent. With a positive action he forced the bottle between my lips and the trickle of liquid gave me instant relief. I hadn't realised how parched I felt, let alone how rough I obviously appeared. I began to suck in more and realised that I had been desperate.

"Woah, Man — not too fast, you'll choke," Gold Chain exclaimed and I realised that I was not behaving well.

"Sorry," I started, but stopped with a startled jolt. It was indeed he who had been on the other train on the night of my earlier experience. In fact I now realised that the vision of beauty was also a part of the same episode and everything was coming back to me. I sat bolt upright with both eyes open and fully attentive. I didn't know where to start and all of my thoughts tumbled out of my mouth simultaneously. "Bow, Stratford, Maryland, Benfleet crash" fell out of my mouth and it sounded as stupid as it really was. "Sorry...."

"Christ, Man, will you stop apologising for just a second and just let me check that you've still got a pulse. You really do look like shit and I think you might even need some proper help."

"No, no, no.... I'm OK.... Honestly." I didn't want to pursue this any further but I did want to know more about Gold Chain. "Don't I know you?" I tentatively started but he was having none of it.

"Just sit back and relax for a minute or two. I think you've had a nasty turn and should just sit still for a bit." He treated me like a naughty school child, although, in my current condition, that was probably appropriate.

So, because I wanted to, I sloped back into my seat and closed my eyes. Only for a second or two, though, because I really did want to pursue my enquiries. My body began to relax and I could feel the adrenaline starting to flow again. I re-opened my eyes quickly but, of course, he had gone. I turned to the people around me for help but everybody was, like all commuters, fully occupied and I knew that nobody ever starts a conversation unless the train breaks down or somebody inconsiderately drops dead. On the basis that I was unaware of either, I reshut my eyes and drifted off into my 'away with the pixies' mode.

A whistle blew — a real steam whistle — and suddenly the sound of pistons barking and the heavy huffing and chuffing of a steam-drawn train woke me. This time, though, I really was awake and I knew that I wasn't dreaming any more. I looked around me and had to look a second time. I was actually sitting in an old single railway compartment with a cushioned bench with six seats on each side. It was jerking and swaying and was obviously travelling fast. The compartment was very full but everybody around me was from an earlier era. At first I glanced furtively but nobody seemed interested in me so I began to examine my fellow passengers more closely.

On the opposite seat, by the door, and obviously feeling a draft, was a youngish chap dressed in an ill-fitting suit that was far too big for him. His shirt collar looked uncomfortable, probably because it was too large, but was furnished with a tie that was too tight and causing him to slip his finger constantly in and out of his collar. I couldn't really see his face because there were about four or five people standing all across the compartment, strap-hanging. The train was rocking quite badly now and some of the standing passengers were struggling to stay upright. I got the distinct feeling that we were in the last carriage of the train — the one that always sways excessively.

The big guy immediately in front of me moved awkwardly and trod heavily on my foot. He tried to turn to apologise but he had large feet anyway and was making matters worse. He muttered a few words over his shoulder but they didn't seem to sound like anything. I was not worried and was about to lean forward and touch him to advise him not to bother when the train lurched badly. It lurched so badly that the big guy went. He fell to his left and took his standing neighbour with him. As they fell to the floor, they both turned to look up, grasping to try to save themselves. I couldn't believe it, for the second guy was Gold Chain again but this time he was wearing a stupid, unpleasant grin that exposed poor teeth and a twisted mouth that seemed to portray deceit. How on earth had he got here?

All of us around struggled to help the two back to their feet but the train continued to lurch viciously and the task was not easy. A large space had appeared where the two men had fallen and one or two of us stood to help them up. Before the space became full again, though, I glanced across the compartment and there, seated prim, proper and upright was Milly with a 'Y'. She smiled at me — I hoped a smile of recognition — but it was so fleeting that I couldn't tell. Shyly, I looked away and instantly hated myself for doing so. She was as beautiful as I had remembered, if not more so but, as I turned back, my view had become obstructed as the two men managed to stand again. In fact I could see only the people on my side of the compartment and the window almost next to me. The window was dirty, I thought, but steam trains had never been anything else.

Still the train hurtled onwards, rocking and swaying violently and still the standing bodies were fighting to retain their upright positions. We flew under a bridge and I noticed that the window wasn't really dirty — it was the weather outside. It was that combination of fog, moisture and breath snatching filth that coal burning fires produced — a proper smog. Another whistle blew and then another one, the second from a different direction, as though in reply. We clattered over a set of points and the train rushed through a dimly lit station, still rocking as though it just had to go somewhere so special and so fast. Maryland. Maryland? So where the hell is Maryland? For the second time in such a short period of time, I felt myself gripping, with fear, everything around me. What was happening to me?

A hand touched my knee — a gloved hand and I realised that it had appeared around the standing figure of Gold Chain. I leaned as far over as I could without falling on the lap of the passenger next to me, a man with a black coat on I think, but I wasn't really looking or interested. I could just catch the eye of the owner of the gloved hand and yes, it was Milly. She smiled sweetly and leaned forward to say something to me. My heart pounded and I longed to hear her sweet tones again.

"Is this the 5:27 or the 5:30?" she asked and my ego was totally deflated — instantly.

"Er, I really don't know," I mumbled and struggled to regain my thoughts. Actually I didn't even know what date it was let alone the time of the train.

"It's the 30th of January, 1958", Milly said and scared the living daylights out of me. How did she do that? I'm sure I hadn't said anything.

Again the train lurched and once again Gold Chain and the big guy got thrown over. This time, however, I ignored them and looked straight across at Milly. She was radiant but I could tell that she was worried. Her pallor reflected fear and I could understand why. As I wondered what to do next, she turned and whispered something in the ear of the passenger next to her. Immediately he stood up and grabbed hold of Gold Chain. With the strength of an ox he hauled the old chap up onto his feet and instinctively I leapt up and started to try to do the same to the big guy. My performance, however, was pitiful and I merely joined him on the floor as the train rocked again. The 'ox' immediately took control and yanked both of us to our feet in a flash and, equally quickly, shoved me into the seat where he had been and spun across the compartment and dropped, as in a well planned military move, straight into my seat.

So there I was, suddenly sitting next to Milly. Would that I didn't feel as though I had the most dreadful hangover ever and was about to throw up. Everything about me was probably repulsive and, at this moment, all I wanted to do was to create a good impression with this total vision of beauty. But I could tell that she was troubled. Her smooth, creamy forehead showed signs of stress. Her gloved hands were clasped together so tightly that I could see the tense veins in her wrists. The rocking of the train had eased slightly but I got the distinct feeling that she was still uncomfortable about it. With trepidation and reluctance, I slid my hand across to hers and gently squeezed it.

"Hey, Milly with a 'Y', don't fret. Look, the rocking has eased off and, besides, you're in the company of friends now." Of what consolation that could have been, I had no idea but she turned towards me and the smallest of glimmers appeared in her beautiful eyes. I couldn't imagine how on earth I had really instilled any confidence in her but she, by comparison, had certainly turned my world upside down.

"I'm sorry to ask again," she started, "but is this the 5:27 or the 5:30? It is very important." Despite my lack of knowledge of which train we were on, I did remember a story my old Dad has once told me about these two trains. He used to catch either, despite the fact that the later one stopped at Benfleet then Chalkwell, missing out his stop, Leigh-on-Sea. But the 5:27 called at Pitsea, missed out Benfleet, then called at Leigh. Since the 5:27 always took a long time to unload at Leigh, the following 5:30 used to crawl through Leigh and many of the commuters used to throw themselves off there regardless. Often my Dad had come home with torn trousers or split shoes as he missed his footing and ended up sinking to his knees, probably not alone. So I thought I understood Milly's issue, although I could not see her indulging in such banal and dangerous activities.

Then I remembered our first encounter — in Benfleet at the scene of the train crash. As I was about to remind her, the woman sitting on the other side of her leaned over and said, "This is the 5:30, m'dear."

"Oh, thank goodness," she sighed and turned back towards me but this time with a relieved smile. Oh, how beautiful she looked. "Could I have my hand back now, please?" she pleaded.

"But of course — I'm sorry — it's just that I find you so, so fascinating.... and very beautiful," I bumbled, still failing to let go. In the crush of the train, I could feel her thigh against mine and I had no wish whatsoever to stop the wicked thoughts that were evolving within my head. "Do you remember me from Benfleet station? You gave me tea when I was in need. You held my head while you administered kindness and tea after the derailment. You were wearing a stunning silk blouse with a high neck and you had white lace gloves," I stuttered.

It was obvious that she had not a clue about any such rendezvous and she was dealing with a troubled man. I tried to think back for further information that might help her remember me but, with a flush of red embarrassment, I suddenly recalled that the crash was in March 1955 — nearly three years before according to Milly. I was definitely losing my mind.

"Oh, yes," she confirmed "nearly three years ago. You called me 'Milly with a Y' just back there and you seemed familiar. I do remember now — our train ran into an empty car on the crossing." Once again she had read my thoughts and this created a level of uneasiness within me. Still I was clutching her hand but this time she seemed reluctant to change that.

The train whistled again and I turned briefly to look out of the window. The smog was much thicker now but the train was picking up speed again and the rocking motion was returning. We roared through Barking under the new flyover and the train began to lean to port as we started the sweep towards Upney. Outside the streetlights of Ripple Road crossing drew dim as the smog grew thicker and again the whistle shrieked. As I turned back to Milly, I could see that she had lost that small level of confidence again as the rocking grew harsher and more frightening. Her hand was now grasping mine fiercely and the twinkle in her eyes had turned to panicking fear. As I turned closer to her she slipped her arm under mine and began to lean against me earnestly. She looked up into my eyes and whispered fervently "Hold me, please — tight — this is going to hurt — just hold me close."

I slipped my arm around her back quickly and drew her into me, just as the train's whistle shrieked urgently several times, as though in panic. I looked past her and through the other window to see the lights of Dagenham Heathway flash past and I could feel her body starting to tremble. She was now shaking so much that I thought she was starting to have a seizure and put my other arm around her stomach. She dissolved into my arms with violent sobs as suddenly the rocking movement jolted with an horrendous crash and the whole compartment reared upwards with bodies, glass and the sound of splintering wood smashing itself all around us. Everything just disintegrated and we were struck from every angle with debris, timbers, bodies and heavy chunks of solid material as the speeding train shuddered, crunched and ground to a halt almost instantly. The complete wall of the opposite side of the compartment, the luggage rack, the seats and all of the passengers just leapt forward onto us along with the few passengers who had managed to remain standing. The whole of the next compartment was surging towards us as well and a concertina effect crushed the whole ensemble, especially us, into the wall behind. Everything was enormous, heavy, hard and unrelenting. But, just as quickly as it started, it all stopped. There was darkness, pain and momentary silence — then there was screaming, moaning and the hissing of escaping steam. Nobody moved. Everything was still for a second and then objects started falling on us.

I could feel Milly within my arms but she was totally still — no longer trembling, shaking or sobbing. I couldn't see if she was hurt or worse and all I could do was lean towards her — so I kissed her on her face. I knew not what part but it felt like her cheek bone. She jerked and turned her face to me. I could just about make out in the gloom her open eyes which blinked. Somehow I was on top of her but there were people and things on top of me. At least we could both still breathe.

"Are you alright?" I enquired and immediately she said "I think so but I can't really feel very much at the moment."

"I think we hit something," I said, stating the bloody obvious but she retorted "Yes, the 5:27 — waiting at a signal in Dagenham East. We must try to get out and help people. There are a lot of people dead and hurt ahead of us. They need our help urgently. We've run into the back of it. Forget our train — theirs is where the casualties are," and we started to try to free ourselves. Who was Milly? Where was she from? How did she know of all these things?

"Milly — I don't know who you are but I want to. Look before we get ourselves out of here and try to help anybody, please understand, I want to see you again. I want to be with you. I want to know all about you. Please, Milly."

As I finished my little impromptu speech, she turned to me again, kissed her finger then placed it delicately on my lips.

"Don't worry," she said, "you've got me for ever now — I shall never be far from you ever again — it is as though I shall be here haunting you, forever present, wherever you go," and then she kissed me lightly on the lips and slipped out from underneath me.

On 30 January 1958 at Dagenham East, in dense fog, the 17:30 from Fenchurch Street ran at high speed into the back of the stationary 17:27 from Fenchurch Street. In total, ten passengers and staff died and 89 were injured — more than 20 of them seriously. Two of those killed were travelling on the 17:30. At least now I wouldn't have to finish those budgets for next year — whichever year it was.

Sinister

RECYCLING

By Trish Gibbs-Leake

Someone is wearing my clothes
Bought from the Charity Shop
Where I handed them to a plumply smiling lady
Who thanked me profusely
Over black bin liner crackle
As I avoided her eyes.
They have folded and flapped around
My stick-insect legs far too long
I have shrunk — not them.

Someone is wearing my shoes
Nicely pointed toes of red
That made me glide, and wobble
When I stood still
Ankles slim, foot arched, blisters burning
High heels clicked on the ground with satisfaction
Demanding attention, announcing my arrival.
Now balance and comfort seduce.

Someone is wearing my smile
I have no need of it
People no longer smile at me
Only hushed voices, whispers, sympathy
"Can nothing be done?" they ask.
Their question makes me want to shout
"No, nothing.... come to my funeral!"

Sinister

BELVEDERE

By Angela Phinn

Kim could see the familiar wooden finger-post just a little way ahead pointing to the right. She indicated and swung her car onto the track, smiling with childish pleasure at the satisfying crunch of gravel under the tyres. At the five-bar gate which straddled the entrance to the sweeping drive, she sat for a few moments hunched over the steering wheel of her car and grinning foolishly to herself as she took in the view, still not quite believing it was all hers. Getting out of her car, she opened the gate, drove through and shut it behind her, then parked at the far side of the cottage, retrieved her luggage from the boot, and took the old, long-shafted key from her jacket pocket to open the front door. The building was long and low; sturdy as a dam. It had been built in 1610 on the footings of an older, medieval building and was surrounded by ancient woodland. It wasn't immediately obvious that it was a two-storey dwelling; what with the low ceilings and steeply pitched roof, the upper floor windows almost disappeared into the tumble of ivy, honeysuckle and roses that garlanded the front of the house. There was a rumour that a cellar existed somewhere under the kitchen, but if there ever had been, there was certainly no sign of it now, the ground floor throughout the cottage being laid with York stone. Additions had been made to the place over the years. Most recently a large Victorian kitchen, scullery, and what was once a downstairs bathroom had been built onto the back of the cottage in the 1880s. As Kim walked through the low doorway, she breathed in the sweet fragrance of the flowers. She almost skipped upstairs and put her suitcase and overnight bag in her bedroom. The cottage smelt slightly musty, not surprising since it had been empty for a while. Kim wandered around upstairs opening all the windows. In the spare bedroom was the black oaken linen chest that came with the cottage, apparently commissioned from a local carpenter by the man who had had Belvedere cottage built. Marigold had told her that the Jacobean chest was always sold with the house and the legend was that any owner who didn't do so always later found they had left it behind. The chest had deep carvings on its four sides and lid. The scenes on the two sides and back were of men tilling the earth, of hunting scenes and of animals, on the lid was a frieze of Belvedere cottage with a man, a woman and a child standing outside the front door which was surrounded by a profusion of intricately carved flowers; but the carving on the front made Kim's scalp creep when she looked at it. It was the image of a man (different from the one carved on the lid) standing in front of a mirror hung on a wall in front of him. His knees were bent as though he were about to fall, his arms flailing and his face a rictus of horror and agony. Below him, from holes in the floor, were many arms reaching for him. As she had looked at the picture, it appeared to shimmer and sway as though moving and she heard a faint, insistent sound like a terrified wailing. She shuddered and felt a draught at the back of her neck. Snapping around, Kim saw the bedroom window was open, as she had left it, but the faint breeze was far colder than it should have been at this time of year, she felt; but then, this part of the house was in deep shadow. She closed the window immediately, grabbed the heavy tapestry cover from the bed and threw it over the chest, promising that she would be rid of the ugly, old artefact as soon as possible — and she would have to get her eyes tested as soon as she was back at work. As she went down the stairs, the fragrance from the flowers outside wafted through the open door and the sun streamed in and her spirits were lifted again. Kim went to her car and retrieved a box from the back seat containing all the paraphernalia for making hot drinks and a packet of biscuits. She checked her watch. The removal men should arrive with her furniture in around an hour, and she was pretty sure they wouldn't pass up the offer of tea or coffee and biscuits. Ah, tea: the oil that made removal men run like a piece of hi-tech equipment. She made herself a mug of strong coffee and carried it around with her, wandering from room to room, peering out of windows, opening and closing cupboard doors imagining colour schemes, building projects and planning where each of her few pieces of furniture might go.

Eventually she wandered back downstairs and began poking

around the rooms. After opening a drawer in one of the kitchen cupboards she was rather surprised, though very pleased, to find an old, unframed photograph of the most recent former owner of Belvedere cottage, Marigold. Judging by the hairstyle of the young woman standing beside her, the picture must have been taken around thirty years ago. Marigold had worn her hair in an elegant bob since she was a young girl. Kim smiled as she took in the image, but couldn't stop tears welling up or the tightening in her throat. She felt so hollow by the gap left when Marigold, who had been such a funny, spirited old lady, passed away.

They had met six years ago. Kim had become a hospital volunteer at her local hospital after her mother had been taken ill and was very well looked after by the nurses and doctors there. She had been assigned to Marigold, who had received no visitors during her stay in hospital so far, and had been told to expect a difficult, unco-operative and unfriendly old woman. Indeed, Marigold was all of these things, but over the weeks, months and years that it took Kim to get to know her, she discovered that the old lady was also funny, intelligent, remarkably perceptive and a great story teller. She had had an unusual and adventurous life, and was so very different from most other people of her generation. Kim, having got the measure of her pretty quickly, had been determined in visiting Marigold three times a week to read to her from books she had brought along. Marigold was equally determined to ignore the 'bloody do-gooder' and would sit with the pages of a broadsheet hiding her face, intermittently shaking it roughly and harrumphing loudly, pretending not to listen. Every now and again she would utter a scathing put down, which Kim found hilarious, much to Marigold's chagrin. As it turned out, Marigold was only a little disappointed to discover that Kim wasn't to be scared off the way most people were after a short time; and so they continued to meet after she left hospital, with Kim and Marigold having lunch together in town every Saturday. Even in her eighties, Marigold was fiercely independent. She was no longer able to drive, so she caught a taxi into town and back again and obstinately refused to allow Kim to either pick her up or take her home. They had known each other a few years before Kim was invited to Marigold's home, "for afternoon tea" she had said regally. It was during this first of many visits that Marigold began to tell Kim some of the history of the house that she had lived in for over fifty years.

The ground on which the cottage now stood, and the ancient woodland was, at one time, a place of worship for an obscure religious sect that worshipped the earth and the heavenly bodies and treated the ancient trees around them with utmost reverence. Local folklore maintained that a wealthy merchant moved into the area who had no understanding of the people and, after bribing the Guildsmen and Councillors of the local town, took over the land by force, razed part of the wood and built the house that originally stood where Belvedere now stood. After the house was completed, the merchant, discovering that the worshippers were still holding their ceremonies in the wood, gathered his men together one night and captured nineteen of the sect. He then locked them in his cellar, which he used as a makeshift gaol. The prisoners were denied good sustenance and fit drinking water, and slowly, painfully they perished, after which the cellar was filled in and boarded over without ceremony. Even now, the locals swore the cries of those desperate people could sometimes be heard. In the years following this barbaric, murderous act, all those involved in robbing the people of their land died mysterious and hideous deaths, culminating in the death of the merchant and his cohorts in a terrible fire at the house. Some years later, a circle of six standing stones was discovered in the woods. The circle had a space as though one stone was missing, but a small boulder was just protruding from the ground. Every few generations a new standing stone was discovered, but always there was space for another one to appear.

When Marigold was ninety-three, she suffered her final illness and she was taken to the local hospice where Kim visited her every day and resumed the old habit of reading to her until the last couple of days of Marigold's life when she was barely conscious and doped up on morphine. It was around four weeks after the funeral that Kim received a letter from Marigold's solicitors. She had been bequeathed Marigold's cottage and one hundred and fifty thousand pounds.

Another thirty thousand was bequeathed to the hospice that had cared for Marigold during the last few months of her life. The antiques in the cottage, apart from the chest, were to be sold and the money raised would be divided between the children of three distant relatives Marigold barely knew. Kim sat in stunned silence for a long while. A five hundred year old cottage and one hundred and fifty thousand pounds had been bequeathed to her? She had read and reread the will, still not having quite taken in the words. She hadn't any inkling that Marigold had any plan to do such a thing! A letter from Marigold was included in the packet that had come from the solicitor. She recognised Marigold's slightly boxy, italic writing on the thick cream vellum. She opened it and read:

Dear Kim,

No doubt, you are very surprised that I have left you my darling old Belvedere and such a sum of money. Well, never having had a family of my own and having spent so many years making sure that no one was able to penetrate my carapace, is it any wonder that I knew no one, nor cared for anyone that I would want to leave anything to? However, you, my dear, without side and with utmost patience and good humour did what no one else could and put up with me exactly as I am (or rather was, considering you are reading this after my demise) and so, why not you? That being said, it wasn't for completely altruistic reasons. I don't want my beautiful cottage (your beautiful cottage) and the woodland that goes with it, falling into the hands of property developers. As I have told you, this land, ancient woodland and cottage is a very special and magical place. I want it preserved, as it is, in perpetuity. Belvedere has survived over four hundred years so far, why shouldn't it survive five hundred years more? And we, my dear Kim, will be woven into the history of the place.

I am aware that, being the young woman you are, you will not appreciate my taste in décor, so of course, I expect you to refurbish and redecorate to your own personal tastes; but I would

83

stress to you that you must not remove or tamper with the old gargoyle in the larder. It is the protector of the cottage and once was (as gargoyles are supposed to be) on the outside of the house; but the old gentleman from whom I bought Belvedere moved him inside after consultation with someone who knew about these things, and as long as I lived in Belvedere, Old Jeremiah seemed happy enough where he is and has never troubled me — not once I found the words in the woods — which you must also do. I'm afraid I can give you no further clue with regards to the precise place these words might be found as, apparently, they will rarely be found in the same place; but if you express the desire, the words will be found. What I do need to tell you, though, is what the old gentleman told me when I bought Belvedere from him: whether you are superstitious or not, please be in no doubt that Old Jeremiah (the gargoyle) is the protector of the cottage. Make friends with him, talk to him and he will not bother you, but take no note of him and he will leave the other spirits that live about the place to make your life a misery and drive you from your home.

I trust that you will not take this as just the ramblings of a foolish, old woman. I ignored these instructions myself, at first, and that mistake almost cost me very dear, indeed.

Well, that, my dear, is all I need to tell you except — enjoy. Perhaps not all: it was wonderful to count you as a friend.

Lots of love,
Marigold

————————×•×•×————————

I put the coffee mug in the sink, and went to the large walk-in larder. On the long back wall were two small windows with frosted glass and a row of air bricks above each of them. The space to the left and most of the back wall was lined with deep shelves. Against the right hand wall was a low, wooden table and on this stood several dusty bottles of home-made wine. I was about to pick one of the bottles up, when I noticed the gargoyle on the wall above me. I could barely believe I hadn't noticed it earlier, but it caught my attention as I saw, from the corner of my eye, the thing seemingly pushed further out of the wall. I just stared at it. The face protruded about eight inches from the wall. It was longer and wider than a human face, and the stone from which it was carved was preternaturally pale. Not a distinct white or cream or grey. It would have been difficult to give an accurate description of the colour: it seemed to shift and change. The mouth of the gargoyle was wide, set in a lipless sneer and its teeth bared or was it a smile? I couldn't tell. The chin was strangely small and pointed with a deep dimple. The nose narrow and hideously cranked upward in an abomination of a dainty retroussé. The eyes, though carved in stone with bored holes for the irises, appeared wild and maniacal, as did the carved hair which stayed still, but at the same time appeared to sway as though in water. Despite my horror, I was fascinated and reached up to touch it, but then he smiled at me. Old Jeremiah smiled at me! I shuddered to my core, and felt suddenly as if I was surrounded by people I couldn't quite see, who laughed and pressed close against me then danced away again just as I turned to face them fully. Somehow though, I could see that their eyes shone with a brilliant, unnatural light; and as I turned and turned about trying to capture a proper look at these people, their laughter rose higher and higher, becoming hysterical. Fingers jabbed at me and frantic hands spun me around. I was exhausted and burning up with heat, my throat dry and cracked. I was so tired. I wanted to sleep. I was sick and despairing. I looked down at my now tattered clothes and as I moved, I could feel the skin on my back tighten and became aware of the welts caused by the whipping I had received. I had been unjustly accused, wrongly punished and abused. Who could I rely on to help me? I wanted to walk in fresh air again and to touch the trees. I couldn't stand up any more; and before I could stretch out a hand to balance, I was falling, falling.... falling.

I awoke on the floor of the larder, cramped in between the wooden table and the wall. My limbs felt straw-filled and I was groggy and bleary-eyed as though I had slept for too long. I looked up at the gargoyle. It was exactly as it was when I had first set eyes on it, except it was stiller somehow. Disjointed images of malevolent, grinning faces and grabbing hands floated across my mind's eye. The sensation of heat and hysterical voices, of bodies pressing close made my hackles rise and fear gripped at my guts. It didn't make sense, not any of it. I managed to get to my feet, albeit unsteadily, and shook my head to clear the fuzziness still clouding my mind. My stomach rumbled noisily; I was very hungry I was. The stress of bereavement, moving and over-tiredness from the last few months had finally caught up with me. That was the reason why I had fainted and had had such a peculiar dream. It was enough to make anyone a bit peculiar. I looked at Old Jeremiah again. It was stone, just stone; and as ugly as ever.

I got myself a plate of cheese and crackers and took it into the sunny conservatory. Just as I sat down and took a bite of my snack, I heard the sound of a heavy vehicle. The removal men! I'd forgotten all about them. I put the plate down and hurried through the house to open the gate for them. The firm of removers were a father and son team from the nearby town. They were funny and friendly, chatting and joking continually as they went in and out with boxes, bags and items of furniture; and it was nice to have the distraction of their presence after the disturbing experience of the last hour. When everything had been moved from the van into their assigned room, I made a pot of strong tea and set down a large plate of biscuits in front of them, and still we three chattered on. From upstairs, there came a heavy thud. Conversation was stilled for a moment before I said "It sounds as though something's fallen over." Ten seconds later came two more thuds in quick succession. I felt the hairs on my arms and at the back of my neck rise in alarm.

I looked at the two removal men; their eyes were wide with astonishment. "I think I'd better go and see what's going on," I said with far more assurance than I felt. "We'll go first", the elder of the two workmen said. I let them go ahead and followed close behind. As we climbed the stairs, more thuds sounded; the noise was coming from the spare room. All at once I felt as though the air had been sucked from the building; as though I were walking at the bottom of a swimming pool. My limbs were heavy; each movement of arm or leg took a gargantuan effort. The two men looked at each other and then at me, and I could tell they could feel it too. An unearthly sound issued from the spare room — the spare room where the heavily carved chest was kept. It was a screeching, growling howl — inhuman.

As suddenly as it came, the thickness in the atmosphere dissipated and the three of us stumbled messily up the stairs. The younger man got to the door of the spare room first and flung the door wide. He had barely done this when a terrified, long-haired white cat streaked past us and out of the house. The tension broke, then, and we looked at each other and burst out laughing. We held our aching bellies and laughed until tears flowed. We trooped downstairs and were suddenly very quiet, each mulling over what had just happened. It was the son who first put his thoughts (what we'd all been thinking) into words; "What do you think that was, then? When we were going up the stairs? I felt like I was walking through treacle or something".

"Nothing but blind fear", his father said, laughing and clapping his son on his shoulder. His son smiled, too, at this; but I could tell by the look in both their eyes that they didn't believe this. It wasn't something I wanted to probe any further; so we just all finished up our third cup of tea and bade each other goodbye.

"I won't forget this house move in a hurry," the younger man said as he leapt into the passenger seat of the removal van. "Neither would I", I thought as I waved them off with a smile still playing about my lips before stepping back into the hall and closing the door behind me. I went upstairs to make a start on arranging my bedroom. The door to the spare room was still open and I noticed that the lid of the chest was open. I frowned with concern and curiosity. How did it come to be open? Surely that poor, terrified cat hadn't been stuck in it all this time, I would have heard it earlier, surely? But if it had been closeted in there, how did it come to be shut inside in the first place, and how the hell had it opened?; and why now and not before? I took hold of the simple silver handle of the lid and closed it. It was, as I suspected, very heavy. Far too heavy for a cat to open on its own; but then, I shook my head as I thought 'Who knows what strength terror can give a creature?'

Kim sat up, suddenly awake. She was sure someone had been shaking her — calling her name. She could have sworn it was Marigold looking twenty years younger and much healthier than she was at her passing; but with a wild and desperate air about her. What had she been saying? She lay back down and shucked the duvet back over her shoulders, then turned the pillow to the cool side. She thought it was something like: 'I told you to speak to him — to Old Jeremiah. For pity's sake there's not much time! All will turn against you. Don't be afraid of him. Look more closely at him and you will see the goodness in him. Speak to him. Find the words in the woods.... Find the words in the woods'.

She had tried to 'find the words in the woods', but there was nothing. What was she supposed to do? What the hell did it all mean, anyway? Kim lay, wide-eyed, trying to understand her dream. Marigold had seemed so real, as though all she had to do was stretch out a hand to touch the old lady's living physical presence, but surely it was just a weird dream, her imagination playing out and processing the days' events? Tomorrow was Friday, the only day that Kim would be working this week. She would go for another walk in the woods on Saturday morning, she decided, and find the words that Marigold had been telling her about. She fell back into a deep sleep.

Kim writhed in her bed as twisted tree roots and branches grew through her mattress making her bed shake and tilt. She grabbed the metal bedstead to stop herself from rolling out and then, whip-like branches wrapped themselves around her arms and legs, tying her to the bed. The room was overgrown with greenery, branches spiralled in through windows and up through the floorboards. Leaves hung in garlands around the curtain poles and over furniture. It was getting hotter and more humid as each moment passed. Kim screamed in terror, but no sound left her mouth. Her eyes wide with disbelief at what she could see. There was a pressure on her chest. Something was pressing down on her. The shape of a man, a man made from the fabric of a tree became clear: he was green and grey-brown, skin striated like bark, twigs and leaves for fingers. He was sitting astride her, pressing down on her chest. Kim screamed again and the sound seemed to shatter the thick atmosphere.

"Leave me alone!"

"Leave me alone!" the tree-man mimicked, a malevolent smirk on his face.

"Let me go!"

"Let me go!" he repeated.

Kim thought to herself: 'I'm dreaming, I know I'm dreaming', but she could feel real pain caused by her bonds. She closed her eyes and struggled to force herself awake as the tree cords tightened around her wrists and ankles. She sat up, wide awake, in her dishevelled bed, her duvet trailing from her ankles to the floor. Her bed seemed to be vibrating — or was it she who was shaking? She turned on the bedside light. She was covered in sweat. 'What a horrible, horrible dream' she thought. She saw a movement from the corner of her eye; and just as she turned her head, she thought she saw several leaves flutter and disappear under the skirting board. Jumping out of bed and shoving her feet into her slippers, Kim stomped off downstairs, muttering aloud "I'm going to find out once and for all what the bloody hell is going on!" When she got to the larder door and saw the strange green light emanating from the gap at the bottom, she thought she would empty her bladder right where she stood. She could hear a faint wailing. Her hands shook crazily as she reached for the door handle, yanked it open and faced Old Jeremiah. "Why are you doing this to me? What does it all mean? What am I supposed to do? I've tried to find the words I was asked to, but I couldn't find them, you must know I've tried. I'll try again tomorrow." She couldn't quite comprehend what she was doing: talking to an inanimate object, trying to talk some sense into it, begging for more time before who knows what befell her. She wearily climbed the stairs back to bed, deciding that when she found the words she was searching for, she would block up the doorway to the larder so that she never had to look at the gargoyle again. "It's not as though I'm actually tampering with the brute" she said out loud.

The morning dawned bright and clear, and despite her tiredness, Kim was up early. As she sat in the conservatory sipping her strong, black coffee, she pondered the events of the past few days and nights. She re-read the letter Marigold had written to her trying to glean more information, and thought over all she could remember of the history and legend of Belvedere. So much of what she had experienced was outside her understanding and beliefs; but she couldn't deny what she had felt and heard and seen, could she? Surely all that had happened were products of her stressed imagination? She thought again of something Marigold had written in her letter: 'I ignored the instructions myself, at first', she had written, 'and that mistake almost cost me very dear, indeed.' That was it, Kim decided. She would put aside whatever reservations or cynicism she still felt and just go ahead and try to find whatever it was she was supposed to find. She put her coffee cup in the kitchen sink and went into the larder to take another look at Old Jeremiah. He was as still as anyone might expect a stone carving to be; no strange, ethereal light, no waving-but-not-waving hair — nothing. Kim went upstairs to take a quick shower before heading off into the woods. She had just got out when she heard her mobile telephone ringing and rushed to answer it.

"Hello?" she said. It was her manager asking her to come into the office. There was an emergency meeting and he needed her there. Yes, yes, he acknowledged she was supposed to be on leave, but they were desperate and no one else was available or contactable who wasn't already in the office. Kim argued and protested, but her manager batted aside each protestation before finally threatening her promised promotion.

"You can't do that!" she blurted lamely.

"Can't I? I wouldn't suggest you put it to the test if I were you", he menaced. "So I'll see you in half an hour", he said, before slamming down the handset. In the end, Kim felt she had no option. There was no way she could find such a well paid job so close to home.

"I'll have a look in the woods tonight or tomorrow", she said to herself as she drove away from the house.

It was dark as she arrived home. She was tired and hungry. Kim grabbed a banana from the fruit-bowl before going upstairs for a shower. As she dried herself, she thought she saw the reflection of the hideous gargoyle in the steamed up mirror. She wiped it briskly with her hand and shook her head at her foolishness. All the same, as she sat in her bedroom, combing her hair at the dressing table mirror, she felt a strange sense of foreboding in the pit of her stomach, and piano-player fingers shimmered up and down her spine. She was just about to get dressed when there was suddenly the sound of wailing, a horrifying clamour of people in distress. Kim's eyes widened and she felt her scalp creeping in terror. She ran down the stairs, taking them two at a time. She was at the entrance to the kitchen when the larder door burst open. Emanating from it was a peculiar green glow. The voices grew louder and as the strange light dimmed, she could see that in place of a stone floor was a metal grille, and through it, bloodied and dirty arms reached and grabbed at thin air. Within the shrieking cries she could make out her name being called. Her legs regained the power of movement and she ran for the outside door. Pelting towards her car, it was only as she stretched out her hand to the driver's door that she realised that her keys were still in the house. She looked back and saw that the strange light was now reaching out into the dark night. She was shaking so hard she could barely stand as adrenalin coursed through her veins. She turned to run up the drive to the main road, but her path was blocked by trees that had sprung up from nowhere. Suddenly, it started to pour heavily with rain. Kim put her head down and ran like fury through the trees towards the main road. As she ran, branches reached down to grab at her hair and arms; tree roots raised themselves from their hiding places to trip her and attempted to curl around her ankles. The faint sound of a car engine in the distance reached her ears. She was crying in loud guttural gasps, almost blinded by her tears and the driving rain. Blood trickled down her legs and arms where she had been snagged by rough bark. She stepped out onto the tarmac and waved at the bright car lights just up the road, thankful that she would soon be on her way out of this nightmare.

The driver could barely see through the rain lashing his windscreen, the wipers barely able to keep up. Not far in the distance, he thought he could make out the figure of a woman; but wasn't absolutely sure as there were no street lamps in this area. 'She must have broken down not far from here', he thought. The figure seemed to stagger back into the trees; but as he got closer, to where he had seen her and looked into the wood, he could see no sign of her, and decided it must have been an optical illusion, caused by the heavy rain and his car headlights shining onto the old wooden finger post.

After carrying the last box from their heavily-laden car into the house, Dan and Jo stood at the front door of Belvedere cottage breathing in the heavy fragrance of the flowers around the door. They still could barely believe their luck at being able to purchase such a find: a large, mostly seventeenth century cottage for less than £130,000. It had been abandoned, so they had been told by the estate agent, by the former owner who had inherited it from an old lady she had befriended; and as no-one had heard from her in six years, the property had been sold by her family who would keep the money in trust in the hope that, one day, she would turn up alive and well. They were cleaning out one of the drawers in the kitchen when they found a letter to the former owner of Belvedere, obviously from the old woman who had bequeathed it to her, judging by its contents. They were neither of them superstitious by any means; but after the chill they both felt at seeing the look on the young woman's face on the front of the old Jacobean chest in the spare bedroom, they decided that they would take no chances.

After lunch, they went for a walk in the woods that also belonged to the cottage, and came across a stone circle. There were fifteen of them in all, but there was a gap where a sixteenth stone might have stood at one time. On closer inspection, they could see that a large, rounded stone was just poking above the grass, looking for all the world like the top of another standing stone. They began strolling towards the other side of the clearing, and just as they came to the edge of it, Dan tripped over a tree root; it seemed almost to reach out of the ground. On closer scrutiny, they saw that a stone tablet was almost buried there and could make out faint writing on the smooth, grey block. Carefully, they pulled away turf and mud and read:

"When ye do count the stones that lie herein,
Then count them thrice, and count them thrice againe.
And ye shall see what pow'r we do wield
O'er land and cot and sod and wood and field.
If you believe we jest and take no note.
Then ere three sunsets pass you will be broke".

Jo and Dan looked at each other, turned back to the stone circle, and counted them all six times. As they left the circle, they thought they could here the faint sound of a woman crying, though it could have just been the wind in the trees.

Sinister

RUN OVER

By Trish Gibbs-Leake

She waited for him to come home
All night
Surrounded by their little sleeping ones,
Straining at every sound,
No sleep for her.

He lay on the road
His long beautiful body twisted,
Stretched out on his side
Not a mark.

At dawn
She laid down her head
And whined.

Sinister

WITNESS

By Paul Bunn

Something woke me.

Sitting up in bed my tired brain attempted to recognise what it was that had disturbed my sleep. Yawning I checked the time on my clock radio; it read 2:35am. I'd been in bed only three hours.

The room was cold so I slipped into my dressing gown, wrapping it tightly around my waist. I was uneasy. Had it been a bad dream or had there been a noise? I didn't want to go back to sleep until I knew for certain. I decided to check around the house; maybe something had fallen off a shelf somewhere.

In less than five minutes I was back, nothing had been out of place. Frowning I climbed back into bed needing to sleep; it was going to be a busy day at work tomorrow and I would be useless without the rest. Closing my eyes I tried to think back to when I awoke. A sound.

That was it! Hurrying out of bed again I went to the window. It was covered in condensation. Wiping the water off with the sleeve of my gown I looked out. The road was quiet; cars were parked on both sides bathed in the orange glow of the streetlights.

It had sounded like a car accident, a screech of brakes followed by a crunch and breaking of glass. There was nothing on the road though and all the parked cars looked intact. I looked to see if it had happened further down but it was clear both ways. Nothing moved except a black cat strolling along the wall of my neighbour's front garden. I was confused now; perhaps it had been a dream after all.

The clock radio blasted out at me and I reached over to hit the snooze button. Peering from beneath the covers I saw a narrow shaft of sunlight radiating through the gap in my curtains and falling onto the foot of my bed. The memory of the disturbance in the night was still there but fading like a morning mist. Throwing back the quilt my thoughts turned to the day's work ahead. I had a meeting at 10 o'clock

97

with the rest of my team and wanted to get in as early as possible to prepare myself.

My mobile rang.

"Shit." I glanced at the clock and saw it wasn't even 7am yet. Who would ring at this time of the morning?

Feeling through my jacket I found my phone, "Yes." Surely work wouldn't want me already.

I was out of the house five minutes later. All thoughts of work banished from my mind, a feeling of panic slowly suffocating me like thick smoke.

"Gina, not Gina."

The hospital wasn't far. I pulled up in front and dashed to the reception desk of A&E ignoring the complaints of those waiting in the queue to be checked in. The young blonde girl at the desk looked at me disapprovingly.

"You'll have to wait your turn like everyone else," she said as she closed the patient file on her desk with a slap.

"Gina, Gina Taylor." I pleaded. "She was in an accident."

The man next in the queue gave me a sympathetic look. "Check for him," he said.

The receptionist typed in her name on the computer after I gave her the correct spelling.

"No, no-one of that name is here. Are you sure she was checked in?"

"Of course I am." I snapped. "I got a call telling me she was at St. Stephen's."

She looked at me warily before re-typing the details. I could see from her face that there was still nothing on her screen.

"Just a minute," she said. I heard a few mutterings of impatience from the people behind me but ignored them. She picked up her phone and made a call. I couldn't make out what was being said but she kept her eyes on me.

Witness

Looking past her I saw my reflection in the mirror on the wall. It could have been a tramp staring back at me with creased mismatched clothing and short, jet-black hair all over the place. With the worry lines deeply ingrained on my forehead it might have been someone ten years older.

I tried to keep calm. Gina could be dead for all I knew and they hadn't bothered to log her onto their system. I drummed my fingers on the desk impatiently as my anxiety grew.

The receptionist finally came off the phone. "I've just checked with the consultant and there has definitely not been anyone of that name in today. I'm sorry."

"This is ridiculous, I want to see someone in charge. You were the ones who rang me." I leaned over the desk my voice rising as my patience finally broke.

"Don't threaten me or I'll call security," she said pushing her chair back.

"I demand to speak to that person you were calling. Don't you understand she's been in an accident and was brought here?" I could feel eyes on me from the crowded waiting room.

"Mr..."

I swung round at the sound of the voice and saw a tall thin man in a suit. A burly security guard stood at his shoulder.

"I'm Dr. Thirwell. What seems to be the problem?"

My anger subsided a little and the panic of earlier kicked back in. "My sister, Gina Taylor, she's been in an accident."

"As our receptionist has already told you no-one of that name has been brought in today." He came over to me putting one long, well-manicured hand on my shoulder. "Now will you please leave."

"But.... "

"No buts, Mr. Taylor," he interjected. "Whatever information you have been given is false." He smiled, his grey eyes showing genuine warmth. "I can assure you your sister is not here."

Wondering what was going on I hurried back to my car and grabbed my mobile from the glove compartment, wasting no time in calling Gina's number. I could hear my heavy heartbeat for the few seconds it took the line to connect.

"Hi Steve."

"Gina?"

"Who did you expect — Kate Moss?" Her gentle laughter filled me with relief.

"Are you OK?"

"Shouldn't I be?"

I didn't know what to say and laughed tearfully yet relieved at the absurdity of the situation.

"Steve?"

"It's nothing." I said. "It's just been a bit of an odd morning and I wanted to see if you were alright."

"Well, when I checked in the mirror this morning there didn't seem to be anything missing."

Same old Gina I thought, always making a joke out of everything.

"Ha! Ha! very funny." I mocked. "I'll speak to you later on this afternoon."

"I thought you wanted to chat now?"

"No, no, just wanted to.... "

"Check up on me?"

I smiled. "Well you are my baby sister." Before she could reply I hung up.

I got back into the car and rested my arms on the steering wheel feeling drained. The call earlier today had been a nasty hoax. How could someone be so callous? I had been totally taken in by it but the worst part was that it must have been someone I knew, or someone with access to information about my family.

My initial instinct was to go to the police and let them track down the culprit. However, I wanted to do a bit of digging myself so I called in to work sick and made my way home. My first call would be to the telephone company.

I couldn't believe it.

"Please check again." I said, my pen hovering over the piece of paper I had torn from the notepad.

"I'm sorry sir but as I've already told you there is no record of a call this morning to your number. The last call was yesterday afternoon."

"There must be a mistake." I tried to keep my voice under control.

"No mistake sir, I've checked and there was no call."

I slammed down the phone in disgust. "Useless bloody phone company" I thought. "They're never in the wrong."

Combing my hands through my hair I sat thinking for a few minutes. If there was no phone trace, then I didn't have a clue how I was going to track down who had done this. The caller had been so convincing, professional and sympathetic at the same time. He had gone out of his way to be positive about her condition even though she was supposedly critical.

My vision blurred as tears sprang with no warning. Gina was all I had in the world. Our parents had been killed in a house fire when we were teenagers. The only reason we'd got out was because the firemen managed to reach us in the bedroom we were trapped in. I could still hear my mother's screams to this day.

Wiping my eyes with a handkerchief I forced the painful memories away, keeping my emotions in check. I sat back in the armchair and closed my eyes. I hadn't realised how badly today's events had affected me until now.

I kept myself busy for the remainder of the day, deciding to catch up with some work on the laptop. My thoughts however were never too far away from the day's events, especially the phone call. Maybe I'd imagined the whole thing. If the phone company had no records then how could it possibly have happened? Worryingly the received calls on the mobile had no record either. The whole day had been weird. It was either that or I was going mad. That last thought nagged uncomfortably at the back of my mind. Eventually I shut my laptop down exhausted, the remainder of my work could wait until tomorrow.

Someone was hurt. I could hear the pitiful cries of pain but couldn't pinpoint the place it was coming from. Darkness enveloped me like a cloak and I couldn't see anything. As I listened the cries grew louder, more insistent. I was rooted to the spot, desperate to help but not knowing where to go.

A deep feeling of trepidation was building inside me. One thing I knew, if I did nothing this person would die. My feet still wouldn't move, refusing to obey my command. Frantically I called out, the cries continued unabated, not hearing my voice. I shouted….

And woke. Sitting up in bed, sweat rolling down my back, I was tense. My eyes were drawn to the window. The echoes from the cries in my dream were crystal clear in my mind. Not knowing why, I went to the window again and, after a brief hesitation, looked out. Nothing!

I realised I was holding my breath and let it out in a long sigh. The street looked as it had the night before, no movement and everything in its place. Again my imagination was running wild. I shook my head; perhaps I should go and see my doctor.

As I turned away something caught my eye. I froze. Slowly I moved back to the window and gazed intently at the road, I was sure there had been a flash of colour there, ever so briefly. Was it a piece of paper blowing in the wind or were my eyes playing tricks in the faint light? At first I couldn't see anything and my frustration grew, then just as I was about to give up the road shimmered. I gasped and put my head against the windowpane to get a better look. The area was quite small, like a heat haze that you see on hot summer days and then it expanded, growing longer and higher until the cars on the opposite side of the road were only a blur themselves.

My hands were cold and clammy as the image crept its way along the road. It got to a length of about 100 metres and then stopped, reaching no higher than a one-storey house so I could still make out the top floors of the buildings opposite. My stomach flipped over and I felt sick. I was compelled to watch.

I noticed the car headlights first. From the right hand side of the haze I could see the beam getting larger as it approached but there was no sound. Within seconds more headlights came from the other direction and from the rapid way the light grew it must have been travelling faster. Where were the cars? I craned my neck both ways but beyond this strange haze there was nothing moving along the street.

I swallowed hard and the hairs on the nape of my neck stood up as I saw the lights merging together. Then the noise began just as two cars appeared from each side of the haze. There was an unidentifiable white car travelling very fast, engine roaring. Terrified my gaze turned to the other side. A yellow car, a mini, had slammed on the brakes but too late. A crunch, the breaking of glass and two heaps of twisted metal.

"Oh…. My…. God." I whispered.

There was no movement or sound from either vehicle. I stood for a few seconds transfixed, then rushed down stairs my only thought to get to those people quickly. The cool night air made me shiver as I ran down the garden path to the street.

I stopped dead at the gate my mouth dropping open in amazement. There was no accident, no twisted metal, no broken glass. I stared down at the tarmac in disbelief; there weren't even any skid marks.

"You are going mad."

That nagging thought pushed its way to the front of my mind like a bully spoiling for a fight. This time it wasn't going to go away that easily.

I couldn't get back to sleep. I was scared. I didn't understand why it had seemed so real; the phone call, the car accident and the dream. I had been working very hard recently so perhaps this was my brain's way of telling me to slow down.

There was one person who I could speak to about this — Gina. We talked about everything together there were no secrets. I could trust her to be honest and give me sound advice. We'd always been close and the fire had brought us closer, it had been our way to get through the trauma. I made a mental note to give her a call in the morning so that we could meet.

I sat at our usual table in The Tavern waiting for her to arrive. She was always late, sometimes up to an hour but it didn't bother me. She spent a long time over her appearance and always looked stunning when we did eventually get together. I was the exact opposite never spending too long worrying about how I looked. Gina always told me if I spent just a little more time on myself I'd find it easier to hang on to my girlfriends.

I ordered a mineral water relishing the cold liquid as it washed down my throat. I was still trying to decide how best to approach these recent events with Gina. Conversation always flowed between us without those awkward pauses that you sometimes get. This was going to be difficult and I was nervous. Gina always said what she thought, which sometimes got her into trouble but at least meant she got straight to the point. I didn't want to be told there was something wrong with me. The thought of seeing a doctor filled me with dread.

"Penny for them."

I looked up startled. "Gina." I stood and hugged her tightly.

"Easy now, you'll suffocate me." She gently pushed me away straightening her dress. "Anyone would think you hadn't seen me for years." The smile on her face could melt anyone's heart, so warm and happy.

"Well, you know when you're late it always feels like it."

She playfully punched me on the arm in fake admonishment. "Next time it will hurt." She said as I rubbed my arm, a pained expression not really masking the smile I was trying to subdue.

"Shall we order? I'm starving."

"Me too."

We sat down and I stared at my menu my smile now gone. The

myriad of meals didn't register at all.

"Steve?"

"Mmm"

Her hand appeared at the top of the menu and pulled it down so she could see my face.

"What's wrong?"

"Nothing, I'm fine."

She gave me her "don't give me that bullshit" look as she fixed her eyes onto mine. I knew I wasn't going to be able to delay telling her.

Putting the menu down I gave Gina a weak smile and wondered how to begin. She could tell I was finding it difficult and gave my hand a reassuring squeeze as it rested on the table.

After I told her everything I felt a weight lifting. Gina only interrupted to clarify anything she didn't understand and listened intently.

Once I'd finished she looked at me steadily for a few moments before grasping both my hands in hers.

"I want you to take a couple of weeks off work starting tomorrow."

I shook my head. "I can't, there's too much on at the moment."

"Steve, I'm worried about you." She leaned forward. "That firm treat you like shit, you need a break."

"Do you think there's something wrong with me?"

"No I don't," she said, each word being emphasised, "but you have got to take time off, that's what you need."

She wasn't going to take no for an answer. Perhaps the holiday would do me good. I was due some leave anyway. Rest and recuperation suddenly felt like a really great idea.

"OK, OK you win." I gave her a quick kiss on the cheek and went back to the menu.

Do nothing. That was all I was going to do with my leave. I'd managed to get the holiday from work but only by hard bargaining with my boss and losing a few brownie points along the way but I didn't care. Wall to wall daytime TV was the limit of my ambition for the following two weeks.

The next time I looked at the clock it was 6pm. Somehow I'd dozed off for a good three hours or so. As I got up from the sofa stifling a yawn the doorbell rang.

"Hi, I wasn't expecting to see you today."

"I've got something to show you." Gina replied. "Come with me." She hadn't been this excited for a long time. I hurried after her as she reached the gate wanting to share her enthusiasm.

"What do you think?"

"What?"

"Look, silly." She indicated the car she was standing next to.

My expectant smile faded as I cast my eyes over the brand new yellow mini she had got for herself.

"No." I whispered.

"Don't you like it?" Gina gave me an uncertain smile. "I got a good deal for it in exchange for my old car."

I suddenly felt sick but managed an "it's fine", before rushing back inside and vomiting on the hall carpet.

Gina rushed in behind me. "Steve what's wrong?"

My stomach wretched again and I steadied myself with a hand against the wall. Wiping my mouth I made my way unsteadily into the kitchen to get some water. My stomach still churned but it was empty now and ached from the sudden convulsion.

"Steve?"

"I'm…. alright." I gulped the water with a trembling hand.

She gave me a long concerned look. "I'll be OK, just let me sit down." I collapsed onto the sofa.

"You need to see a doctor, you look terrible."

"Thanks." A smile barely registered on my lips. Gina perched herself next to me, mobile already against her ear. I had no strength to argue and felt weak, the beginnings of a headache already pressing against my skull like a vice.

This was ridiculous, basing my fears on a mirage of a yellow mini in a car crash, it must have been a figment of my imagination. But I felt a sense of certainty though, as certain as night follows day.

The doctor came and went, not finding anything wrong with me. It could have been something I ate or possibly brought on by exhaustion. In other words he was hedging his bets. He recommended complete rest for a few days.

"Do you still think about the fire?"

Gina had busied herself clearing up after me and making a snack. I wasn't keen on anything more than buttered toast as my stomach still felt delicate. It was a shame because Gina was a great cook and made a mean lasagne, my favourite. She sat opposite me on the armchair, the food already a memory with two plates of breadcrumbs on the coffee table between us.

"Most days," I replied, "it's not that easy to forget." I rang my index finger around the glass of water Gina had given me, feeling uncomfortable that the subject had been raised. Even though it was ten years ago, the memory couldn't be forgotten. Most people had good memories of their parents, remembering the good days, going on holidays or picnics. Mine were filled with fire, panic and screams.

Gina studied me carefully, her short blonde hair silhouetted in the lamplight behind her.

"How's your boyfriend Alex?" Changing the subject would help, anything to move away from that memory of our past.

"He's fine, as gorgeous as ever. He's taking me to his parents' at the weekend."

"Not popped the question then yet?".

She shook her head. "I think he will though."

"Steve, there's something I wanted to ask you." Sitting forward she clasped her hands together as if in prayer, all trace of humour gone.

"This sounds serious." I tried to keep my expression neutral; wary of what was coming next.

"I've been thinking about the fire recently and how Mum and Dad must have suffered." Her voice cracked on this last word and she quickly went to her handbag to retrieve a tissue.

"Gina…"

"No, it's alright I want to tell you."

"I went through some of Mum's personal stuff. I know we said we would keep them as mementoes and not go through her things, but I did today and found this."

She handed me a letter addressed to Mum. It was a small white envelope, torn at the top where it had been opened with one sheet of paper inside, neatly folded. It was handwritten on one side. I read it with rising incredulity, surely it couldn't be.

"There are copies of her replies as well. So it's true."

Barely able to stop myself tearing it into tiny pieces I read through it again. I didn't recognise the handwriting; thin and spidery, barely legible. It felt like a knife through the heart.

"I had no idea, Steve. It was a complete shock to me as well."

"Show me the reply."

Quickly she fished through her bag and gave me a similar letter.

I placed it on the table after reading it my mind numb with shock. How could she?

Those words repeated themselves over and over again. An affair, and it was crystal clear that they were besotted with each other, the passion jumping off the pages with its intensity. I'd always thought Mum and Dad were so happy.

"Did you have any idea about this?"

"Not until I read them myself." She folded the letters up neatly and put them in her bag.

"That's partly why I bought the mini, to take my mind off it."

"Do you know who he was, this Mike Jobson." I could barely bring myself to speak his name. All my childhood recollections of family life now seemed tainted and false.

"I've never heard of him. It just seems so wrong to me. I could never imagine Mum having an af…"

We sat in silence for a long time, lost in our own shattered memories.

Despite the maelstrom of emotions within me, my mind was trying to work out why she had been in love with another man. What problems did they have? Did Dad know? What with this and the strange events of the last couple of days my once comfortable world was falling apart around me.

Gina had silently put her coat on and was about to leave.

"I'm sorry for dumping this on you now especially after what has happened." She sighed heavily. "But you can see why I shared it with you."

Opening the front door she stopped and turned.

"I'm just as confused as you are." Her eyes reflected the sadness we both felt. "We'll talk more about this later."

My sleep was dreamless except for the voice. The tone was urgent almost demanding but no words were discernible. I listened intently but it soon faded, becoming a whisper lost in the dark recesses of my troubled mind.

Rain splattered onto the kitchen window with such ferocity it sounded like tiny stones. I barely tasted my breakfast cereal, pushing the bowl away after only a few mouthfuls.

My childhood was a lie. That thought was growing like an aggressive form of cancer, eating away at me piece by piece. I slammed my fist down on the table with such force the cereal bowl flew off the table and smashed on the floor. Thunder rumbled in the distance.

The kitchen grew darker as the storm clouds approached.

At first I didn't notice anything, I was lost in my own world, everything blotted out, but then I heard it. A soft scratching sound, at least that was my original impression. Looking around, now alert, everything seemed to be in place although the light was so dim from the storm that I couldn't be sure.

Then it was there again and it sounded nearby. Shivering and feeling suddenly cold I moved around the table and heard a crunch as I stood in the mess spilt earlier.

"Bloody hell." I looked down and froze, my heart skipping a beat.

The pieces of my bowl were still moving laboriously, allowing a pool of milk to stand free in the middle. Tiny waves appeared causing the milk to shimmer like a miniature sea. Then gaps cut in to the milk through to the floor underneath. At first there was no pattern to them but it soon became clear that they were words.

I shut my eyes willing this latest strange "event" to go and not come back. The words were still there a few seconds later.

"Stop him" they read.

A ragged breath escaped from my lips, as I stood terrified. The pieces of broken china became more agitated clicking together like chattering teeth before rising up. They began to rotate; slowly at first and then as they reached head height faster and faster until they became a blur. A scream like a banshee arose from the middle of this storm, so loud that I covered my ears the pain unbearable. Just as I thought my eardrums would burst the noise stopped as suddenly as it started, the china pieces falling to the floor like hailstones.

It was a few moments before I was sure it had finished, my ears were still ringing. There were no words written in the milk, which had now spread into a number of smaller pools.

Part of me wanted to run, get out of the house and not stop until I collapsed from exhaustion. Things were happening and it couldn't all be stress related. Thunder roared loudly, much closer than earlier and I glanced at the window. There was another message written into the condensation, already water droplets were running down the letters making it look like the messages you see in blood in the old horror films. My legs were like dead weights as I crossed the kitchen to double check what it said.

"Not safe."

―――――×•×•×―――――

David Kempton laughed again, wiping the spittle from his bottom lip as he watched the house. His friend of the last few weeks had been talking to him a lot. David had always been lonely and felt awkward in company. In his youth everyone had kept him at arm's length saying he was "weird"; those who did get close he found had just used him, mostly to borrow money and not pay him back. He hated them because of that. He'd never met anyone he was comfortable enough with to call a friend until now.

First of all it had just been a brief conversation here and there and most of the time he ignored it, wary of being used again. He was never pushed though; if he didn't want to talk it wasn't a problem and if he did then that was fine as well. Gradually he became more confident and felt something he'd never known before — trust. That was when his friend told him the secret and what he must do.

Part of him was scared because this was the first time that anyone had asked him to do something like this. However, his friend had said it was VERY IMPORTANT and it would make him happy.

His dark brown eyes glazed over as he went over it in his head one more time.

Watching the words slowly dissolve on the window I knew I had to do something. Going to the police wasn't an option. What would I tell them anyway, that I'd had phantom phone calls and visions of a car crash, which may involve my sister. They'd take the first opportunity to smile sweetly and lock me up before throwing away the key, another lunatic wasting police time and money. There was Gina to consider of course. Whatever was going on she seemed to be the focal point. It was her name that was mentioned on that call and I was certain it was her new car that was in the "accident".

Someone (or something?) was trying to get a message across to me. There seemed to be a hint of desperation because it was happening so regularly.

The signs in the milk and on the window had rocked me like a sledgehammer blow. Everything that had happened to me was a warning; it wasn't a fantasy of my own making. Staring outside the raging thunderstorm matched the frantic activity in my mind. Pieces of the jigsaw buzzed around but didn't quite fall in to place. Growing frustrated I snatched a pen and notepad off the coffee table, maybe writing it down would help.

GINA
PHANTOM PHONE CALL
ACCIDENT
NIGHTMARES
WARNING
LOVE LETTERS

I paced the dining room, occasionally glancing back at the paper on the table. I needed to concentrate on coming up with a way of preventing this disaster.

Eating buttered toast was all I could manage again that evening. My note from earlier was still in front of me but with an addition. It didn't seem related at first but the more I thought about it the more certain I was it should be included. My eyes had been fixed on it ever since my pen had finished the final letter.

FIRE

———×•×•×———

She hadn't told him everything.

Gina sat with her feet up on the settee mulling over her conversation with her brother earlier. It had been a bombshell to her when she had found out about her Mum. She hadn't wanted to go through the old letters that had been left when she died. They were Mum's own intimate words to their Father and it would not be right to intrude on what they said about one another. But something had changed. It had been a long time since her parent's death and there had been a void that was never properly filled. Reading the letters had seemed a way of getting into their thoughts again, understanding how they felt about each other. Perhaps it was a way for her to lay their parents to rest after they had been wrenched away in such tragic circumstances.

Now she wished the letters had just been burned or thrown away. There was a lot more in them than she had bargained for. Should she tell him?

Sighing heavily Gina picked up her wine glass and took a sip, savouring the taste of the red wine in her mouth before swallowing. Placing it gently back onto the table she came to a decision. She would tell him but not yet. Steve needed to rest for a couple of weeks; he definitely wasn't himself at the moment. Once he was back into his normal routine she'd take him out for a meal and break it to him gently. She was going to need time to plan how to tell him although she didn't know how.

Switching on the TV she tried to take her mind off it — if only for a while.

In the library going through the archived newspapers detailing my parent's death was a painful experience. Looking at the charred remains of the house, even with the pictures in black and white was extremely difficult. The stories in all the local rags were quite short, with very little detail, just saying how tragic it was. The general consensus of opinion was that it was accidental, caused by a burning cigarette. Both my Mum and Dad had smoked all their lives. After scanning through the newspapers for some time I realised there was nothing new that could help me here.

A gust of icy wind bit in to me as the first few drops of rain touched my face in tiny splashes. Running to the car I sat behind the wheel gazing out at the gunmetal grey clouds scudding across the sky. What more did I expect? The fire had been an open and shut case so why spend time looking for something that wasn't there. And yet...and yet, I now sensed there was. Frustrated I made my way home.

Dropping the car keys onto the table just inside my front door I heard the familiar beeps of my answering machine. It was Gina.

"Hi Steve it's me... I need to speak to you about Mum's letters. There's something else.... something I didn't tell you. Come round as soon as you get this.... please".

I was straight out the front door again. Gina had sounded different from her normal self. There was a thin and trembling edge to her voice. Racing through the streets my knuckles were white from my hands vice like grip on the steering wheel. My heart filled with dread at the thought of another secret being revealed about my parents. I couldn't understand why she hadn't told me the full story before. Nothing could be worse than what I already knew about them. The only reason she must have held back was if it was worse. The way Gina had sounded I feared it would be very bad indeed.

Gina's flat was up on the first floor and it was in darkness when I arrived. Having my own key meant getting in wasn't a problem, but this wasn't right. Gina always had most of her lights on at night. She was afraid of the dark and had been for a long time.

Hesitating outside her door I listened: silence.

"Gina."

There was no sign of any movement. My hand was shaking as I slid the key into the lock and entered the flat, the door squeaking as it always did. With heart thudding hard in my chest I felt for the switch and turned on the light. Blinking at the sudden brightness and stepping in to the lounge everything was in place but still no sign of Gina.

"Gina are you here?" My voice sounded dry and paper-thin.

The kitchen was tidy except for one thing. A half full cup of tea stood on the breakfast bar, lipstick smudged on the rim. What caught my eye though was the folded piece of paper sitting under the saucer. Hurriedly I grabbed it.

"41 Franklin Drive. Get here by 11 if you want to see Gina again — alive. No police. It's that simple. I'll be watching... "

"Jesus." I whispered.

My foot barely left the accelerator as the adrenalin coursed through my veins. I lost count of the near misses I had on the way but didn't care. Someone had got Gina and whoever it was must know about our past. A trickle of sweat ran down my neck as terror probed at the deeper recesses of my mind. I needed to keep control and with great difficulty managed to stop it from invading me completely.

41 Franklin Drive. I didn't need a map to get there. It had been indelibly printed in my brain since childhood because it was where we had lived, and where our parents had died, all those years before.

Franklin Drive was one of those streets where you knew rich people lived. There were long driveways with large houses at the end of them, some hidden by trees or large hedgerows. Many had ornate gates of all shapes and sizes with impressive names across the top. I remembered standing in front of some of them as a child and marvelling how grand they seemed. In that respect, number 41 was no different from the others, except in one vital way. No one had bought the house since the fire. It had immense structural damage so maybe the cost had been prohibitive.

Approaching the rusting gates I noticed they were ajar, the padlock broken. A shiver ran through me, I had been here only three or four times since the fire and the memories always came flooding back. With some hesitation my hand clasped the cold iron and pushed. The gates screeched complainingly as they moved inwards. A gust of wind blew into my face and a dust devil spun like a mini tornado at the side of the gravel path leading to the house, the leaves within rustled like a bird's rapid wing beat.

The light from the streetlights was bright but I still couldn't see the house until about 20 metres further along the gently curving driveway as it veered left. Even then it was masked to some extent behind a row of brooding oak trees. The house's blackened shell stood like a huge skeleton behind the once beautiful garden now overgrown with weeds. Only a small portion of the roof remained with many climbing plants worming their way up the walls on all sides. Any windows that weren't broken appeared like the black lidless eyes of a monster. Gina's bright yellow mini was parked outside the open front door.

Spurred on I dashed into the gloom not aware of the shadow that launched itself at me. I felt pain on the back of my head; then there was darkness....

The smell was the first thing that hit me as I stirred groaning with the mother of all headaches. Trying to raise my hand to the back of my head proved impossible as they were tightly bound. A whiff of a long dead fire was all it needed to bring my focus back to where I was.

"I'm so pleased you could join us Mr. Taylor or shall I call you Steve?"

The man stood in the dim candlelight leaning against a dining room chair which had Gina gagged and bound to it. Her beautiful hair was now plastered to the side of her head and her face contorted in pain. It was the eyes that got to me though; the normally vibrant, confident look now evaporated leaving despair. Swallowing hard I turned towards our captor.

Of average build and height, with a mop of untidy blonde hair he wasn't what I would have imagined a kidnapper to be. The six-inch knife he held to Gina's neck though was the only proof I needed to see that he meant business.

With a great deal of effort I pulled myself into a sitting position. All the while he watched me, a humourless grin spread over his face.

"I'm David Kempton — you can call me Dave if you like." It sounded like an introduction at a business meeting.

"Why don't you put the knife away? I can't exactly jump up and overpower you." I said.

He appeared to consider this for a moment before gradually lowering it. The relief on Gina's face was evident.

"Well this is lovely and cosy isn't it.... back home?" David began humming to himself, still with that inane smile. His eyes appraised the room we were in which had once been the lounge. As a kid I remembered it was huge with wooden flooring and an oval green patterned rug as the centrepiece. My father had had a bookcase built at the far end, as he was a lover of books, buying two or three every month. It's also where my fondest memories were.

"What do you want?" At that he looked at me as if I was stupid, then burst out laughing, a real belly laugh like when someone tells you a hilarious joke.

Eventually he calmed down. "Oh Steve that was soooo funny."

"What?"

He saw my lack of comprehension.

"Oh, of course you wouldn't know would you?" He walked around behind Gina and I saw the fear in her eyes as she watched him. For one second I thought he was going to kill her as he brought up the knife to her head. My hands fought with the knot around my wrists but I was helpless. With a sigh of relief he simply cut off Gina's gag.

"Go on tell him." The spitefulness in his voice made me wince.

Only then did I notice the angry red mark around Gina's left cheek. He'd hit her. My arms wrestled with the restraints again with renewed vigour — I wanted to kill him on the spot.

"Bastard." My face felt hot with rage.

He laughed again but there was no merriment in his eyes, which just stared back at me with utter contempt.

"Steve.... "

"Are you ok?"

A weak smile crossed her lips. If only I could reach out to her, say that everything was going to be fine. She was my baby sister and I had let this happen. At this precise moment I hadn't a clue how we were going to get out of this alive but put on a brave face for Gina anyway.

"Tell him or so help me I'll cut out your tongue." She let out a short scream. The knife was held just a few inches from her throat.

"You see Steve she has a little secret." He began circling her like a vulture over carrion. "Well, not just a little secret but a great big, whopping one."

He stopped by her side and gently rested his hand on her shoulder.

"I'm not your sister." At first I thought I'd misheard as the words came out in a whisper. Clearing her throat she repeated herself so there was no misunderstanding.

Confused I said nothing, thinking she must have been forced to say this, a cruel joke to add to our misery. There was no time in my life when I was without Gina so it couldn't be true. "Is this what you brought us here for, to torture us, to tell us lies?"

My hands had pins and needles; even moving them around wasn't helping.

"What? You don't believe her?"

"Steve it's true I'm not." The imploring look she gave me made my heart shudder. "I haven't had the chance to tell you." She glanced fearfully at our kidnapper, "until now."

"There, that wasn't difficult was it." David pinched her cheek playfully ignoring her brief cry of pain as he touched the now significant bruise. "I've got to get some supplies from the car so won't be a mo." As he strode towards the door he stopped and cocked his head appearing to listen. He sniggered and mumbled something indistinct before continuing.

When he'd gone I staggered to my feet. It took me two attempts, and the room wouldn't stop spinning. Standing still for a few seconds I waited to regain some focus before trying to walk. Despite the questions I had my overwhelming desire was to get nearer to Gina and give her what comfort I could. Although I knew what she'd said must be true the reason I was still here now was because of her. Through thick and thin after the fire we had always been there for each other and no one could take that away from us.

"Don't worry we'll get out of here." I said this with more confidence than I felt.

She smiled back, tears still at the corners of her eyes. "Of course we will."

David got to the car and opened the boot, all the time listening to his friend.

"You know what you've got to do."

"Yes, yes," David replied eagerly. "Of course." Sometimes his friend seemed so impatient. They had gone through it many times so how could he forget. Everything had gone according to plan so far and they couldn't go anywhere. It was running as smooth as clockwork as he'd promised and David would always keep his promises for his one and only true friend.

"What name should I call you, sir?" Ever since they had first met he'd never thought to ask his name until now, leaving it as "sir." He'd never met anyone he could relate to before. Now emboldened by what he had done the time felt right.

He was greeted by silence. Panic rose inside of him and he almost dropped the "supplies" he was carrying. He didn't want to be alone again in this world that hated him as much as he hated it.

"Robert."

He held his breath.

"You can call me Robert."

Tears filled his eyes and ran freely down his cheeks. Feeling that the final hurdle had been overcome now that someone had finally accepted him he strode confidently back into the house.

Not knowing what to look for didn't really help us with an escape attempt. There are no books entitled "How to escape from a madman when you and your sister are tied up" so I didn't really have anything to go on. I sat back on the floor and gave Gina my best "keep your spirits up" smile. She was staring intensely at me.

"Who is this maniac Gina?"

"I don't know, he only turned up this evening. I've never seen him before." She tried shifting position in her chair but the binding was too tight. "He knows everything though." She said this last sentence more to herself than me.

The trembling in her voice made me want to reach out and hug her, tell her everything was going to be fine. She appeared on the edge of the abyss and I had to stop her going over. Although the situation we were in was desperate and my mind raced to find a way out, I also wanted to know more about what she had told me — a bombshell in any other circumstances.

The room was gloomy, the once bright and happy house that this had been was gone forever replaced by a rotting carcass that died along with my childhood when the fire took hold.

"Tell me the rest."

Straightening in her chair she began, hesitatingly at first but becoming more confident as the story unfolded.

"Remember those love letters I showed you the other night." I nodded, feeling sick at the thought of them. "Well, there were a lot more in Mum's things, a hell of a lot more."

She paused, gathering her thoughts before continuing.

"About eighteen months before I was born Mum and Dad went through a difficult patch in their marriage. Dad was working longer hours and sometimes at the weekends as well."

"That's hardly an excuse." The words left my lips before I could stop them and I instantly regretted it. The bitterness I felt towards Mum in that instant was hard to control. Gina was biting her trembling bottom lip as she spoke.

"I'm sorry Gina, I know it's not your fault." She looked at me with a mixture of guilt and understanding.

The thought of Mum with another man just filled me with disgust. A lot of marriages go through a rocky stage but manage to work through it. Having an affair was the easy way out.

"Would you believe they met in the supermarket." She attempted a smile but it turned in to more of a grimace. "You know, the one that's just down the road."

I nodded, remembering it well.

"Mum had a huge shop to do as it was approaching Christmas. Dad was away as usual and with you at school she wanted to get as much of the shopping done as possible."

"How do you know this?"

"It's in the letters Steve. When they wrote to each other, which was all the time, every detail of their relationship seems to have been

120

included." She shook her head in disbelief. "It's as if they were telling their story."

"Anyway Mum had a trolley load of food and was struggling to get it to the car. He offered to help her and they started talking." She winced at the pain her bindings were causing. I could sense the difficulty she had telling me this but urged her on wanting to know everything

"So what was the attraction? People aren't normally picked up in car parks."

"I wasn't sure at first." She hesitated, unsure as to how to carry on. "But then, I found a photo." She looked at me directly, confusion dancing in her eyes. "My Dad, apart from having less hair and being a heavier build, looked like your Dad."

"Are you sure it wasn't our dad?"

Gina seemed to miss the sarcasm in my voice; her eyes were unfocused as if lost in thought. "No it wasn't, I'm sure. You see there was one other feature he had which showed clearly on the photo." She shuddered. "He had two fingers on his left hand missing."

A shadow out of the corner of my eye caught my attention as David came back carrying a large bag.

"He lost those in prison you know; machinery accident supposedly." The sneer in his voice emphasised accident. For a few moments he rifled through his bag ignoring our presence.

The silence felt threatening in the emptiness of the room as I wondered what he had planned. My concern for Gina had made me forget all that I had been shown and led me blindly into this spider's web. As I watched him lift out the contents of his bag my worst fear was realised. Gina screamed.

"Please carry on." David stopped what he was doing, a cheerful smile on his face. It gave no comfort to either of us. "Gina has got more to say you know."

I now understood what he was going to do with us. Tears were streaming down Gina's face, a mask of terror and desperation. I needed to buy some time and the only way I could do that was to get Gina to finish the story. I still had no idea what to do to get us out of here.

"So the attraction was that he looked like Dad." Gina didn't hear me at first, her eyes hypnotised with what our friend was doing so I repeated myself, louder this time.

She slowly turned her head, eyes re-focusing in my direction.

"They were brothers."

I was barely able to draw breath: Brothers? From all the memories I had of my parents there was never any mention of a brother. I'd always thought that they were both single children.

"That can't be right. We would have known."

David started laughing again.

"Ooh you haven't heard the best bit yet." He said when he was able to control himself. "Wait till you hear the rest."

Gina began to tremble, loud sobs escaping in gasps. David was over to her in a flash, knife poised on her cheek. Stroking her hair he whispered in her ear, an evil grin on his face. With eyes as wide as saucers she stared at me, a silent pleading for help.

"Leave her alone you bastard." The rage spilled out into a roar as he pricked her skin with the knife and a trickle of blood ran down her face. "I'll kill you for this."

David just looked at me like an insubordinate child.

"Really, I'd like to see how you manage that given your.... situation." With a sudden lurch he got to his feet putting the now blood stained knife inside his coat pocket and went back to his work.

Gina appeared not to have noticed the cut; her attention focused on me. I could see the effort she was making in trying to shut out the horror around us.

"Brothers…" Gina's voice was a whisper as she continued. "He'd been in prison for killing a man."

I still found it hard to believe, even now. "But why did we never know?"

"Because he was ashamed." David stared at me through his dark

122

impenetrable eyes, his voice a growl. "Ashamed because he didn't believe it when I pleaded my innocence."

David's face seemed to blur in the faint light of the room as he spoke, but it passed almost as soon as it had begun. A finger of fear wormed its way into my stomach. "What do you mean you pleaded your innocence?"

Turning to face me his features began to shift and ripple and I knew it wasn't my imagination. "Exactly that." he said.

I was struck dumb by the vision before me, no longer did I see David's face, it had changed somehow into one much older, rounded with a large bulbous nose and uneven teeth. The eyes, although slightly larger were the same dark bottomless pools they had been before. A large unsightly scar ran down his right cheek. The rest of David's body remained the same.

"Dad…. ?"

Gina's quivering voice cut through the air as this monstrosity gave me a humourless grin. I wanted to scream but my throat felt like sandpaper, unable to make a sound.

"That's right, Dad." He appeared amused at this insight, nodding his head in approval. "Robert Taylor."

Wind suddenly gusted through the ruins of the house making low moaning sounds as it roared through the empty rooms. This thing, even if it was some sort of incarnation of Dad's brother, did not deserve that nametag.

"Why did you have an affair with Mum?"

There was silence for what seemed an age. I could hear water dripping somewhere nearby, magnified by the stillness of the night outside.

"Because he'd ignored me for years. How do you think I felt when I found out that he hadn't even told his wife or son he had a brother?" His accusing eyes bored into my skull like a drill, fixing me as a snake does before it strikes. Moving closer he grabbed my face with his hand

and held the knife up in front of me. "Well?"

He pushed me away in disgust when I didn't answer. Holding my breath I tried to steady my galloping heart and regain some composure.

"But why...." I started.

"I'd been in jail and he was a witness." The words cut through the air. "Your father, my brother, sent me to prison." Bringing his hands to his face he studied them carefully. "He said he was ashamed of me for what I had done, but he should have protected me." He snorted dismissively, "And he knows it."

Delving into his pockets he pulled out a box of matches. An excited grin crossed his face. He'd finished talking now and was eager to finish the job he'd come back for.

He lit the first candle his eyes gleaming in the firelight. "In less than an hour you will be dead as you should have been all those years ago."

Moving on he lit the others — six in all. The petrol he had poured over the floor from the cans now smelt overpowering. I was desperate, not for myself but for Gina, she didn't deserve any of this.

Calmly David/Robert sat in between us and closed his eyes. "Now it ends."

I watched as the candles slowly burned their way to the petrol stained floor feeling helpless and contemplating a death that I could have suffered all those years before.

Robert Taylor was at peace. He had found it so easy to take the body of this man, someone weak willed and simple to manipulate. For too many years he had been lost in the darkness, bent on revenge against his brother but impotent to do anything until the right person came along. It was going to be so sweet watching them burn and hearing their screams. Already he could hear the pitiful cries of David Kempton pleading to be allowed back into his body. Well, as the saying goes don't trust anybody whether friend or relative. He threw his head back and laughed. Not long now.

My thoughts snapped back into focus with the laughter breaking in to the deathly silence. I felt no fear now, just an inner calmness, which was totally at odds with our situation. Surely I should be shouting and screaming fighting to get away but I wasn't. There was a heightened awareness to my senses, every object was clear; there were other smells apart from the petrol; the dampness of the rotting roof timbers; the sweat from my body. As the room temperature dropped like a stone a certain thought ran through my mind repeatedly. A tear came to my eye and I smiled. I could tell by Gina's face that the same thought was occurring to her.

Something was wrong; why were they both smiling? They were going to die for Christ's sake, but there was no terror on their faces, just a stupid grin.

"What are you smiling at?" Standing in the candlelight I could see the angry pulse on the side of his neck.

"Just remembering my parents." I returned his gaze. "Mine and Gina's real Mum and Dad. The ones who loved us and cared for us until you killed them."

Turning to Gina she gave him the same stare. "So was I."

His knife was out in a flash, but before he could move something strange happened, something wonderful. Dad appeared directly in front of his brother, who stood transfixed as if caught in headlights. My heart leapt with the sudden shock and joy of seeing him again. For a few seconds nothing happened, like the respite before a storm hits, and then came the scream.

It was like nothing I'd ever heard before, a cross between a human scream and a lion's roar. My blood froze. David/Robert brought the knife down over and over again onto Dad, wailing continually, but it had no effect, going straight through him. Dad's ghost shimmered with the onslaught, almost disappearing on several occasions but it didn't move.

"Stop!" The voice was loud and commanding. I'd never heard Dad speak in this way. Even when angry he had always spoken in soft, even tones and there hadn't been any time when he had raised it.

David/Robert stopped mid-strike, breathing heavily with sweat pouring from his face. "I think there has been enough suffering, don't you dear brother." David/Robert just stared back, hatred emanating from every pore. "You're no brother of mine."

Dad appeared to straighten at this, his face hardening. "What you did was unforgivable." Robert just laughed, a cold heartless sound full of contempt. "Do you know what? She deserved it."

Dad's face filled with fury, his whole ghostly figure glowing even brighter.

There was something moving in the corner by the fireplace, an oily black mass writhing in on itself. It stretched up towards the ceiling, not reflecting any light; absorbing it like a black hole. A pair of red, hungry eyes appeared within it, watching the conflict with keen interest. Without making a sound it moved stealthily towards them.

"Dad." My warning came out as a whisper but he heard, saw the approaching apparition.... and smiled.

Robert didn't notice until it was almost upon him, pouring over his body like a blanket. He ran screaming from the room, the black mass covering the top half of his body, terrible wet ripping noises coming from within. Moments later he was gone and the room was silent again.

The tension in the air drained away and Dad's ghost diminished until it was a mere outline although his face was still clear. It hit me then how much I missed him, the lump in my throat threatening to bring on tears. Gina watched him, her love for him clearly etched in her gaze.

Dad first went to Gina, placing a delicate hand on her head. She closed her eyes as a bright light enveloped her body and then in a blink of an eye was gone. She was free. Slowly she stood, wincing at the pain as the blood started flowing to those parts of her body that had been tied.

"Thanks Dad." She said. His aura glowed brightly at that. His elation was clear but I also detected sadness there. He then came to me.

"Son, there is something you need to know." His voice was now thin and watery as if coming from a long distance.

Freeing me, as he had Gina, I waited while flexing my hands. Part of me didn't want to know what he was going to say, but wanting to know anyway.

"I did witness Robert killing a man. He strangled him over some petty argument in the street after we'd been to the pub." He cast his eyes down, as if ashamed at this admission. "It was the hardest thing I ever had to do, giving evidence against him, but it was the right thing to do, brother or not." I could see he had no regrets about the decision but that it still hurt him that he'd had to do it.

"I couldn't tell your mother about him." His shoulders sagged. "Although now I wish I had."

I wanted to hold him right then, tell him everything was fine and none of this was his fault. The agony of his confession pulsed from him in waves.

"He started the affair as soon as he left prison, determined to get back at me for what I did." His figure wavered as if blown by a breeze. "If only Carol had known who he was." He sighed with regret, shaking his head slowly.

I felt some of the bitterness return. "She did what she wanted to do."

Dad's eyes blazed for a moment before he regained control. "That's true. I was never around enough and when I was he wrote to her using an alias, Mike Jobson. You see he was covering his tracks even if the letters were found."

Thinking of what they wrote to each other again made my blood boil. "It's not an excuse Dad. You had to work and you worked hard."

"And what about the fire? It wasn't an accident was it?" Gina came up beside me and held my hand tightly.

He closed his eyes. "No it wasn't. Robert started it because Carol ended the affair."

"Mum did?"

"Yes and he hated me even more for the fact that in the end she chose me over him. That's what sent him over the edge I think, he committed suicide a week later." He came closer to us then and I could feel the essence of what he had been in life, a decent man trying to bring up his family. I reached out to touch him my mind a whirl of emotions.

"He spent a long time planning the fire, waiting some years after Gina was born so he could make sure every member of the family suffered."

"But what about me, why didn't he want me?" Gina interrupted. "I am his daughter after all but he hated me."

Dad looked at her, the emotions on his face unreadable. "I brought you up because.... " For a moment he was lost for words. "...You were conceived after the break up."

"So she went back to him."

"NO."

"Then what?"

Dad looked from me to Gina, the conflict within him evident as he eventually settled his gaze on Gina.

"Oh Gina, my sweet. My brother.... He.... raped her as punishment for breaking up with him. You were the result."

For a while no one said anything. I went to Gina and just hugged her.

"Why didn't you go to the police?"

Dad didn't answer at first, his expression one of regret. "Carol didn't tell me for three weeks and was terrified of going to the police."

Eventually Gina removed her tear-stained face from my shoulder and looked up at me, she was smiling.

"Do you know something." She was sniffing and wiping away the tears with her sleeve. Her beautiful eyes were shining brightly. "It doesn't matter and do you know why?"

"She pointed to the wavering figure of Dad. "That's my real Dad over there."

    At that moment all hell broke loose.

There was a sudden flash and I felt heat against the side of my head. Rolling onto my side I saw that one of the candles had burned to the floor, flames were leaping up, consuming the fire damaged furniture. I ran to Gina who was already on her feet.

    "We've got to get out of here, the whole place is going up." Gina looked at me, a crooked smile on her face.

    "Didn't you hear him a few minutes ago?" Grabbing her to me tightly I remembered his soft, but certain voice in our heads. "When you were kids I said nothing or no-one, would ever hurt you. Don't worry, I'm here."

    And we knew he was.

    Running from the house we were laughing as more fires ignited like hell itself behind us. I could see the relief in Gina's eyes reflecting how I felt. My life now had a clarity that had been missing all these years. I was sure, now, that the painful memories of my childhood would never haunt me again.

    When we were clear of the house I saw the mini disappearing down the drive with David/Robert, or what was left of him, at the wheel. His scream was like nothing I'd heard before, a pitiful wail that stopped me in my tracks. Blood was all over the windscreen; so much I couldn't believe he was still alive.

    Another pair of headlights appeared from around the bend travelling at great speed. There was a screech of brakes followed by the breaking of glass and crunching of metal. A thought struck me and I stared at my watch. It was 2:35am.

Sinister

DÉJÀ VU

By Trish Gibbs-Leake

Doris had had a fine day
There had been a visitor
A lovely girl
Fair hair and and shy blue eyes
Just like her own.

They'd talked of this and that
She'd brought some grapes
The black ones
Doris especially liked
And flowers
She wondered why?
Baby pink carnations
Her favourites
What a bit of luck!

Doris tried not to complain
About her daughter
Who never came
And never bought her
Flowers or grapes.

She tried to remember
The girl's name
But couldn't — oh well!
Funny to have a visitor
A stranger
On her birthday.

Sinister

THE MARK ROYCE CHRONICLE

By Simon Woodward

30th December

Over the last nine days I've been gradually becoming aware of, but not really taking that much note of, strange visions; visions of shadowy folk in the periphery of my sight, only to turn and look and then see nothing. Because of this I've generally assumed that they're floaters, bits of debris that we all get in our eyes, until now that is.

The events of today have disturbed me somewhat and this is due to the fact that, this time, when I turned around, I got a brief glance at a fully formed shape which then disintegrated in front of me.

This last experience has pushed me into thinking I need to start a journal, just in case something happens to me. Not that I think it would, I mean, why would it? But just to be on the safe side I will have an account of the whole saga, if and when it unfolds. Perhaps I'll publish it, if it ever gets finished, who knows?

31st December

Well it's New Years Eve and there's not a lot going on for me.

Today I sent an email to senior management telling them that what they're trying to do (which is nothing in my opinion), is totally crap. I think I may lose my job because of this. But then who cares, they really don't know what they're doing, so, why shouldn't I say?

Went out with work tonight to drink in the New Year. Pretty tedious evening, nothing special, same old, same old. Oh well let's see what the New Year brings.

1st January

It's 3:30am and I am back here writing, trying to capture what has happened between leaving the party at half past midnight and now.

I'd only been asleep for a while when I was dragged from the blissful respite of dreamlessness to fully conscious!

It wasn't anything to do with my other half, (I don't have one), but because of the Shadow-folk wandering about my place. This is new; I've never seen them here before, it's only in the streets near my flat. They are without noise. I think it must've been the drop in temperature that woke me.

They show no acknowledgement of my presence but, once I'm awake, they're something I can't ignore.

I was shivering in my bed even though the heating was on. And they were just wandering about. So I'm up and typing away. Apart from my disturbed sleep there is just them; wisp-like things, irrelevant.

I'm going to get the extra duvet and go back to bed. I'm glad the thought of ghosts doesn't bother me one bit, they're harmless, it's strange how most people don't realise this.

Here we are again and guess what? New Year's day is crap. Nothing going on, nothing is happening. No one wants to know, none of the local pubs are open. All I have is the telly to watch.

8pm now, telly is rubbish, the usual regurgitated stuff and that's why I'm writing again. Somehow the telly turned itself off and the radio turned on. This doesn't worry me; occasionally it happens to everyone doesn't it? Anyway it's probably due to some kind of electrostatic disturbance created by sun flares or something.

Tired now, going to bed.

2nd January

Been to work, same old shit, I suppose its saving grace is that it keeps me in beer money.

3rd January

Work was acceptable, went home via the local watering hole, and then left at the dictated time.

About half an hour ago I was woken. It is now 3:30am (again). I've decided to get up, or at least get out of bed and add to this journal.

They've been back, the Shadow-folk that is. I've only been able to see their ghost-like presence. They're hard to describe. I mean how would you go about describing something as intangible as individuals, I assume they're individuals, made of smoke. This is not just your ordinary smoke however but the kind of smoke that burning tyres produce, thick, black, and almost transparent in places. And in writing this description it has made me realise they're more here, physical I suppose. Not like before. They've changed.

I've been up for hours now, it's 6am. Apart from the noise they've started to make, which is new, they've disappeared.

I'm going back to bed; at least I'll get one hour's sleep before the alarm goes off. Best do that, I can't afford not to.

4th January

What a crap day. I'm surprised I functioned at work at all. So tired. Glad I made it through. Avoided the local, was too tired. It's now 8pm, I'm going to bed. Please, please, please don't disturb me tonight.

5th January

Been to work; what an amazing day. No problem with the email I sent. Management are OK about it, sort of, but at least I haven't got the sack. Best not do that again though.

I slept right through last night without any problem. Don't know whether I was visited, but if I was, I was not woken. It'll be great if I can get another night's sleep, just the same as last night.

Good TV tonight. I am certainly going to relax, may well crack a few tinnies.

6th January

It's bloody 3am and I'm up again. They're back, wandering about sighing, moaning. I am truly getting pissed off with this. What have I done to deserve this? It's bloody 3am Friday morning. This is too much. I've got to do something about this. The novelty has worn off. I'm fed up with having to tell my mates that they can't visit. And I want to dispel the idea that I am a total saddo.

What the hell was that?

For the journal, something has just crashed heavily in the hall I'm going to go and have a look.

Can you believe it nothing has crashed anywhere? I walked along the hall, dodging the Shadow-folk, and there was no sign of anything. What was that noise? God I'm tired. I'm going to have to be more proactive about this. Problem is I just don't know where to start. I think this Saturday I'll try the local library to see if that throws up any pointers. I dearly hope it will.

5:50am now and they've gone. Off to bed, looking forward to waking in and hour and ten minutes so I can get up for work (not).

Been to work, fortunately it was not too taxing, but I am, and was, truly knackered. The guys wanted me to go out to the pub "as it's Friday". So I didn't disappoint.

Surprised I'm still able to type; one or three too many beers and I could hardly keep myself upright which was strange as I didn't have that much. Not tired anymore though: probably the expectation of being woken. Best have a few scotches to see if that solves the problem.

7th January

I didn't get up until 11am. What a good night's sleep.

During the usual chores one has to do as a single person I mulled over the other night's visions trying to glean any clues from the memories. With hindsight and without the fear, which is becoming more tangible, I did notice things that are sort of familiar with the

Shadow-folk. I think they were dressed in woollen clothing and most wore cloaks but that's as far as I can recall at the moment.

I'm off to the library now.

Well there wasn't much help there; loads of general stuff about Essex and the Normans, a little bit about the Romans, no detail though. And nothing about Manor Mews, which is just off Manor Lane (where I live). Anyway that's what the local library had. So helpful. Actually I'm being a bit mean, I did find a book with some pictures of Celtic clothing that rang a few bells and the librarian did suggest trying the Internet. Don't know why I didn't think of that in the first place, working in I.T., as I do.

Typing again, it's 8:53pm according to the PC clock and it has been a pretty standard Saturday, apart from the library visit. No calls from the guys. Looks like a night in. I think I'll just pop around the corner and pick up a DVD, perhaps Altered States with William Hurt, haven't seen that in a long time.

Nearly 12:30 in the morning and the film was as good as I remembered it, the cans of cider were a good complement. Good night all.

8th January

I've been up now for about twenty minutes, the coat stand in the hall was on the floor. I expect its crash woke me and yes the bloody smoky apparitions are back having their fun. I think I only slept for about two and a half hours.

I'm really fed up. I've got to find out why this is happening. I can't go on like this. It's doing my head in.

I'm going to watch to see if they give any clues as to why this is happening. The time now is 3:47am

Well that was interesting, the ghouls/ghosts, I don't know what to call them, Shadow-folk is probably pretty accurate, mainly appear in the hallway. Some of them seemed to come from the airing cupboard. The rest just mill about as if they are not sure what they're looking for. Can you believe it?

Anyway, I decided to open the airing cupboard door for myself. You won't believe this but the emersion tank was no longer there, neither were the shelves, neither were my pillowcases or duvets or anything, just a very dark landscape. I think I saw a tree off in the distance; it had no leaves just scrawny and twisted branches. The earth was dark brown perhaps even scorched, I think, and grassless as far as I could see.

Whilst I was standing there, I heard a sound. Straining my ears I could just about hear something. It was almost like hundreds of people screaming in sheer terror. No. Not people. Souls seems to be a more appropriate description. Not that I can say I've heard screaming souls before but their cry imbued such a resonance of feeling, my soul and spirit, in the deepest depths of me, was almost crushed by their out-pouring. To be quite honest I had to shut the airing cupboard door a lot faster than I opened it. This situation is becoming very hard to deal with.

The time's coming up to 6am and silence is now pervading. I need to go to bed. I need to pretend that this is not happening. I need to be away.

Just got up, I've washed etc, it's now 1:37pm. Nice sleep but what a waste of a day.

I really have to find out what this is all about. The local library is not that good, as you may have gathered. If I want to get to the bottom of this I'm going to have to trawl the Internet, but what do I search for? I hope my supposition that the answers do lie somewhere is correct because if they don't, I'm really worried about my sanity. I know I've just got to keep going and hold on tight to my belief that there is something that will explain this; something documented, something that I can get to grips with to help me finally figure out this problem of mine.

Why no one else in these flats seems to be bothered by this problem I don't know. Perhaps they are. I've not actually asked them, but if I do and they're not, what then?

Just come back from my sister's place. She's as nutty as ever, which is fun, but fancy her being a doctor and as daft as she is. Brother-in-law is just the same as he always is, fit, straight forward and without strange happenings. Didn't actually mention what is going on in my life at the moment. Perhaps I should, perhaps I shouldn't. Who knows?

Oh well, I'm going to sign off now and watch a bit of telly (as usual). The Time Team is on soon and I hope that'll take my mind off things for a while.

Dear Journal,

I'm off to bed now. I really hope we don't have to meet up again in the next ten hours, but if we do, then I'm glad you're here and that you will not judge me.

Goodnight dear Journal, thanks for your help.

All the best

Mark.

9th January

What a beginning to a new week. Management have decided to address the problems that I highlighted earlier and they've asked me to direct the ongoing upgrades. I don't think I've mentioned this but I'm the company's internal I.T. consultant of sorts, probably not.

Anyway this has nothing to do with the new found strangeness of my life that I'm attempting to capture in this journal.

Got a big presentation to do tomorrow. All the European management team will be there. I'll have to finish the final touches tomorrow morning, most of the work I finished today.

10th January

The presentation went exceptionally well. We all know what has to be done. Everyone is happy with the year's plan. Let's hope it actually happens.

Not wanting to tempt fate but I've had two trouble free nights on the trot! Is it all over? I hope so.

Going to sign off now and watch a bit of telly. One question bothers me though; will I get a good night's kip tonight? I want one, but I am cautious in my optimism.

11th January

Work was great, again!

You've probably noticed that I didn't add to my journal in the morning. I mean who has time? I don't, I don't even have time for breakfast, mainly because that means I'll have to get up earlier.

Crap telly tonight so I'm going to watch my Dune video, been a few months since I've watched that. A damn good film if I do say so myself.

Hello, I'm back. Went to bed thinking all my woes were over, but guess what, it's 3:05am and I've had to get up and add to this journal. The bastards are back. They haven't touched me but now I have smashed pictures on the floor of my lounge. Their manifestation seems to be becoming more real, more physical, a true presence in this world, my world. This is not good.

The noises are worse; in fact they are terrible; the screams just pass straight through my head, piercing, wrenching screams.

The airing cupboard door has been flung open and the soil I saw before is alight, burning. Black smoke is billowing above the unreal scenery.

When I look out of my study towards what was the airing cupboard I get glimpses of withered, skeletal things writhing in the agony of the flames. The individuals I see are covered in a burning light. Their clothing, I think it's their clothing, is dropping off them, forming flame ridden puddles, flickering orange and red.

Others mill about with no interest in helping their own. Now they look towards me, mouths agape, seemingly yelling, seemingly imploring me to do what, I don't know.

How I'm keeping myself together I have no idea. It's almost as if I have been through this before, I'm used to it somehow. But how can that be? How can I cope with this presentation of hell on earth? Why does it not affect me to the degree that I would expect others to be affected? This is truly unfair; most people would have surrendered their consciousness by now. Is this not correct? I am forced to be an unwilling witness to the trauma of these Shadow-folk. What has it got to do with me? Why has it got to do with me?

Before I could walk amongst them not too concerned. Now I'm stuck to my chair in sheer terror, watching, feeling reviled, as some burn in abnormal flames and others just, just... it's so hard to describe, just mill about ignoring the pleas of their own kind. I am desperate for release from my unnatural participation. I don't want to view it any more, but it keeps going on and on and on. I try shutting my eyes but I still see. I see limbs dropping from bodies alight. I see blackened skulls, mouths open in screams of total pain as the smoke, or is it steam (?), pours forth out of the darkened orifices of their faces and all the while the flames lick greedily around the oval of their skulls. NO MORE PLEASE!

12th January

I don't know what happened for the rest of the time since my last entry.

It's morning now and I must have passed out, thank God.

I've phoned into work saying that there has been a family bereavement and that I won't be in. This will give me a few days grace.

It's only 8:30am and I'm going to bed now. I need some rest. I hope the memory of the previous night does not interfere.

13th January

No problems last night and no work today. I'm feeling a little better.

It's strange to note how a decent night's sleep can make you feel.

It's times like this that make me question the reality of the previous weeks' experiences. Everything now seems so normal. Have I just imagined the whole thing? Is it an overactive imagination that is causing me these problems? At this moment in time this is exactly how I feel, what a stupid imagination. But when I look about my lounge and see the smashed pictures of my family, I just shudder.

No, I haven't cleared the mess up yet and this is only because I fear that if I touch those broken pictures, those pictures of my family past and present, it will bring the Shadow-folk back to test and taunt me again.

Just back from shopping. I don't know whether you, the reader, have realised this but it's Friday the 13th. God help me.

I'm certain that, if anything terrible is going to occur, it just has to be tonight. Who invented Friday the 13th?

It's only 4pm and I'm trying to think of ways that I can knock myself out for one purpose only, and that is to allow me to forgo the traumas of tonight's inevitable visitation.

It's not as if I can go out and avoid the whole thing. Nothing ever happens until the early hours anyway.

Back from the offy; I've a full bottle of Famous Grouse and twelve cans of Scrumpy Jack. Oblivion is not far away I hope. It's now

6:35pm and time to start my journey towards blissful annihilation before anything can happen. Cheers.

14th January

4:47am and I'm typing once more. This is the first time I've been able to get back to the journal and add this entry since I was awoken by some invisible presence dragging me from my bed, from my slumber.

I think it started around 2:30am.

I got into bed after completing half a bottle of scotch and four cans of cider, 10:15pm I believe.

At about 2:30am I was dragged, by my neck, out of bed into the hall. I remember trying to recoil from the strong fleshless, tinder dry fingers around my neck, but I couldn't, fear had paralysed me. I was pulled onto an unnatural earth and dumped, let go. From then on all I could do was watch, and even though the experience of being physically manhandled was worse than the previous were, I felt calmer. My fear probably muted by alcohol, I suppose.

The hallway, including the airing cupboard, was no more. What lay before me, and under me, was damp brown earth with gloomy green hillocks just visible in the distance.

Night was wrapped around the land holding the darkness fast, just as it had previously when I looked on from the other-side.

In front of the hillocks were wattle and daub roundhouses with a few cattle in a paddock off to one side.

A trumpet, of sorts, sounded. But it wasn't a trumpet, as you and I would truly know it, the noise was something more akin to the noise a bass wind chime may make, being blown continuously.

Some men emerged from the roundhouses in front of me, about 100 metres away. They seemed very worried. Their women appeared, leaving the roundhouses. Those with children were holding them close to their bodies covering the children's ears against the eerie sound.

Then there were two floating fireballs on the brow of the hill and a regular clump, clump, clump sound forced its way through the viscous night air, perhaps the sound of many feet on soft earth walking(?)… marching(?) in unison(?).

The little peace that was left was then shattered.

The men in their hide(?) coveralls ran to each of the roundhouses ushering out the remaining women and children, screaming at them in some language or another, to go, directing them away from the oncoming... I don't know what.

Then silence and there was nothing apart from the lowing of cattle and the occasional cry of a child. The air was still. No more clump, clump, clump, no more eerie guttural wind chime.

When I looked back at the men they all had their swords drawn and were facing the raised ground, facing the hillock behind their huts looking at the floating balls of fire. The women and children had gone.

While I looked on, wondering what was going to happen next, the men talked amongst themselves occasionally pointing toward the hillock. There was a tension in the atmosphere which was almost palpable.

The silence of the night was interrupted by a light whistling sound, a sound which imperceptibly increased in its intensity.

All of a sudden the roundhouse, just in front of me, cracked loudly as its roof disintegrated and its wooden uprights supporting the roof were smashed to pieces. The wall fronting the roundhouse opened up in an explosion of daub and straw, as a burning rock exited.

Cattle went mad and crashed through the willow fences that had contained them. Then there were more light whistling sounds, more loud cracks, more huts were smashed to oblivion before spontaneously erupting in flames.

I tried to get up but for some reason my legs were not responding. It was as if I was not completely of this terrible world; part in and part out. I tried rolling to my right and this worked, I rolled over and over until I was out of the line of fire. I stopped when I could roll no more. I had ended up next to a pile of rocks. All I was now able to do was to watch the ongoing destruction of the settlement.

In the flickering shadows cast by the floating fire on the hill top I could see one or two hide covered individuals beckoning to the soldiers(?), beckoning for them to make their way further into the settlement. This was very confusing and before I could think anything else of it, another projectile came out of the sky and smashed into the rock-pile in front of me. The rocks fell upon me.

That's what I remember from the last two and a bit hours.

And now I'm back here attempting to put, on paper, the memories of what had just happened.

Everything in my flat is quiet again and the airing cupboard is just that.

Not feeling well today, totally shattered, feeling so tired. The early hours of this morning were grim. This situation has got to me so much that it has made me vomit. I want it all to be over.

15th January

Resting, that's what I'm doing today, resting. I need to rest. My mind is still reeling from the other night's forced excursion into that bleak world of fear and resentment.

I try to make sure I keep adding to this journal though I have no energy to do so.

It's difficult to get back to the computer; my legs still feel as if they're not with me.

If I cease to exist at least there'll be something, some explanation why, something for my family and friends explaining my demise/disappearance. They will have to take this journal on face value. I hope they don't think this is just the ravings of a non-descript person, their brother, their friend, who lost his mind and disappeared for reasons unknown.

Yes. I am certain now, that there will not be a good outcome to this. I am resigned to my demise.

I've just come off the phone from my boss. I've told him that my family bereavement has affected me more than I thought it would. He has said that within the company rules I can have another 3 days off. I thanked him and said I would be back on Thursday.

16th January

Bleak as the last few days have been I am beginning to feel OK. Not brilliant, just OK.

After re-reading my journal from the 13th, which was very difficult, especially so soon after the event, I think I have understood where I ought to start looking to understand why these awful visitations are happening.

I remember the people in their animal skin clothing, the wattle and daub homesteads and the foot soldiers. These things are all pointing to a Romano-Celtic era. Why I'm being torn from the present and dumped in this awful manifestation of pre-history, I have no clue.

But at least I can feel fairly confident about the "when" of it. I don't just watch Time Team, I do listen as well!

And however much I wanted an insight, I could have done without this baptism of fire.

At least now I have my seed, my kernel, the beginning of my understanding. I truly hope it's the beginning. And I pray my understanding will deliver, at the very least, an explanation.

I'm going to log on to the Time Team forum and ask a few questions; things like how do I find out about the history of my area, who can I contact for more information? I hope that the people in this forum will respond and give me some idea of what to do next. Not that I'll let them know why I'm asking.

Well I've done that, logged on, set myself up on the forum and asked the questions. All I need to do now is wait. I hope their answers aren't a long time coming.

Going to watch a bit of telly before I go to bed.

Hopefully, tomorrow, I'll be able to sign on to the forum and get some guidance.

17th January

Gooood morning Haaadleigh, that's Hadleigh, near the sea, actually. Decent night's sleep, had breakfast already and it's still only 9:45am!

Received a strange letter post marked Italy; its contents knocked me a bit. There was one sheet of paper containing a single sentence, "I will avenge my family." It wasn't signed. Is it my imagination or are there really more loonies these days? Anyway I threw it away.

Once I've finished this little entry in my journal I'm going to sign on to the Time Team forum. I really hope there'll be some answers to my questions.

Well, well, well, some answers. In order not to bore you with all the information the bottom line is; call the "Sites & Monuments Record Office, County Hall Chelmsford." Apparently they're the best place to start. Any enquiries regarding ancient goings on in my area they're the people to ask. This is good, I'm feeling the most positive I have in a long time. 'scuse me while I get on the phone.

Oh well, a little bit disheartened now. Spoke to a nice young lady called Sarah who told me that she wasn't the best person to talk to for the details I was after.

However she did say that her colleague, "Janus", was the right person but his shift did not start until 3pm, "would I like to call back?" I said "of course" and thanked her for her help.

This gives me about four and a half hours before I can do anymore so it looks like the hoovering is beckoning.

It's 3pm, I'm going to make the call.

The call was very peculiar, so much so, I'm going to have to enter it in this journal just as it happened.

"Hi. Can I speak to Janus please?" I said.

"This is Janus speaking." Was the reply.

"Good. I have a few questions, did Sarah tell you?" I continued.

"No." Was the response I got, which was a bit surprising to say the least.

"Oh! Do you have some time?" I always ask this because I'm never happy intruding on anyone's time.

"Yes. What is it you want?" The man called Janus said.

"Well, my name is Mark Royce and I would like to know a little about the area I live in now, especially relating to its history." I informed him.

"Mark Roize? Is that spelt R.O.I.Z.E?" At this stage I was truly unsure of where the conversation was going but carried on anyway.

"No, it's spelt R.O.Y.C.E. Does that make a difference?"

"Yes."

"In what way?" By this stage I didn't know what was going on because I'd phoned to ask questions not the other way around.

"Where do you live?" Janus went on.

"I live in Hadleigh, almost opposite the Norman church. Now, as to my question…"

"Do you live in Manner Lane?"

"Yes. And now, can you please tell me why the spelling of my last name has any relevance? Actually how the hell do you know what road I live in?"

"Because I have some information you need, some important information that should put a stop to your current predicament." By now his stance was beginning to rile me.

"My predicament! What the hell do you know about my predicament? I don't know you from Adam, I've just made this call and there's no way you can know me. I'm sorry you're talking total bollocks."

"Sir I implore you... just listen for a few minutes"

Well, against my better judgement I listened and when he got to the bit about his spirit guide I just turned off until he finished.

"And that's it?"

"Yes, please take my advice."

"Thank you Janus. I'm sure we won't be speaking again." That's when I put the phone down.

At that stage I went into the other room and put the telly on, I was fuming, vowing never to take any notice of Internet forums and assuring myself that tomorrow I would seek out other lines of enquiry.

Suffice it to say, after watching the box for a bit I'd calmed down and got to thinking it was possible that there may have been an essence of truth in what he was saying — no on second thoughts probably not.

I'm thankful for you, my journal; it certainly seems to be a good way to get things off my chest. It makes me calmer, apart from the typos I am continually struggling against.

But it can be said that it is better to have typos to thwart than the demons of a bygone age. Where am I getting to now? Am I becoming some kind of philosopher or something? Best not worry about this.

OK, it's only 7pm now so I'm going to do something normal and put a DVD on. I think I'll go for Blade Runner.

18th January

It's just gone 12am and there is a fairly intense smell of smoke. It's triggered something in my head. It's not your usual kind of smoke smell, like paper burning or rubber, something else.... something that I remember deep down.... something I can't quite put my finger on at the moment.

Obviously I've got up and turned the computer on to write this, but there's nothing to see, nor hear, just the smell.

Sitting here waiting.... it's an awful feeling. Not knowing what is coming. I hope nothing.

Just waiting and waiting.

I think now is a good time to get a drink, probably scotch, before the next mind wrenching episode. Something to help me deal with what is to come. (I pray to God it's not, not coming that is.)

Got the scotch from the kitchen now. Not a glass, I've got the whole bottle. 'scuse me while I have a slug.

The worry is getting to me again. I need to throw up, my stomach is churning.

The smell is back, that acrid, awful smell, it's so much stronger now. It vaguely reminds me of pork in some way, perhaps a bit sweeter, but burnt pork at that, not truly burnt sweet smelling pork, but almost.

Still no sounds, just the smell. I think it's getting stronger, if it isn't my imagination making it so.

Just so you know, I'm sitting here at my computer with a bottle of scotch and everything I do is illuminated by the computer screen.

I haven't turned the lights on because if they return I just hope they'll miss me, not see me.

Sitting in this darkness, being anonymous in the blackness, helps me focus on getting everything written down.

I don't want my peers or my family thinking I've lost the plot, someone they no longer want to be in contact with. So I write and wait.... and wait.

Oh no, it's started, I'm awake again, I must've dozed off. The clock on the PC says 2:14am. The airing cupboard door smashed open violently (I assume it's the airing cupboard again, I haven't looked yet) and I'm awake. No noise though, complete silence, the clock on the wall no longer ticks. I can not hear the fridge making its usual sounds. There's just me and silence in the glare of the monitor's LCD backlight.

My vaguely illuminated hands hover over the keyboard.

I'm finding it difficult to type, I'm afraid that any movement will bring them straight to me. I am pressing the keys as slowly and as quietly as I can, struggling to override the fear that wracks me, that attempts to paralyse me.

Oh God how I wish this was over.

It's no good, I've got to look. I can't take the silence and the smell any longer. I'm going to look.

And I will. I just need to lean forward a bit so I can see out through the door of my study, into the hall and towards the cupboard, and now I've seen it, it's a cupboard no longer, more of an entry into Hell on earth, I think.

From my study I can see the scorched soil is there again but still there is no sound, no Shadow-folk either.

But.... I now hear an estranged noise growing, getting louder in its intensity. It's a unified noise, a unified chorus of voices growing louder, a chant.

"Animus" they say, "Animus" over and over again.

I am oddly thankful that the silence has been broken and, along with it, my total fear. I think I let my imagination go in the forced immersion of silence.

I must get more information, something that will lead me to understand the situation I am in.

I'm not going to wait until the chant sounds as if it is in my flat. I'm going to cross the threshold and move into that other world and see what I can find out.

I pray that this is not the last entry into my journal I ever make.

19th January

What has happened? My head feels like it wants to split open. I can hardly type but I need to. I need to write my diary. 19th, where did the last twenty hours go?

The pain in my head, what happened to me? The pain in my head is too much.

Pain, pain, pain.

2nd February

The geezer from the flat below, Dave, has brought my laptop in to the hospital. Didn't really know him that well but he must be a decent sort.

He said he hadn't noticed me out and about but my car was still there. Not on holiday he assumed.

Apparently he called to check on me, after work had sent someone round to find out what I was doing. All they did was knock, and having no reply, they knocked on his and asked if he'd seen me.

Still feeling dozy, but thank god for Dave, he found me.

After the person from my work left, he forced open my front door, and there I was, unconscious in front of my computer.

After the ambulance had got me to the hospital I apparently came round long enough to tell the doctors about the things that had happened to me over the last few weeks. They told me that everything I had felt and seen, the hallucinations, the weakness, the tiredness, the smells, my bouts of anger and rage, were all classic symptoms.

The doctors rushed me to have a brain scan and found a tumour, benign, thank God.

Now I'm sitting here in bed, bald as a coot, feeling a bit woozy.

If it wasn't for Dave, goodness knows what would've happened, I'm glad he's a perceptive chap. The fact he brought my laptop to the hospital, means to me, he must have read my journal and understood what I was attempting to do. The best thing is that he hasn't mentioned anything about the entries.

Keeping up these entries is tiring, I'm worn out now, so I won't add any more today.

3rd February

Feeling better. Can't wait to get home. The food here is awful. Not sure when I'll be allowed to leave.

Not a bad bed though, got an excellent view of the grounds. Right next to the window I am. Don't like lying around though. I'm in my own side room, which is good. Not much in it, just a TV, a cupboard that could do with replacing, and no en suite.

I think it must be midday now. The winter sun is shining through the window.

—————×•×•×—————

The nurses have just informed me that it's lights out in a few minutes. This doesn't mean I have to stop typing on my laptop but I will. They tell me I need the rest. Been through a major operation I have, but it's a good day tomorrow, I've been given the OK to go home, can't wait.

Just woken up, don't know what disturbed me, it's dark and silent. For some reason the door of the cupboard is open.

I'm starting to breathe faster; I can feel trickles of cold sweat running down the middle of my back and an insuppressible sense of terror welling up inside me making the skin of my scalp feel like its being pulled taut. The hairs on the back of my neck are now prickling. I am suddenly chilled to the bone.

The hell of the last few weeks was all down to the tumour.

They assured me it was. It was; wasn't it?

4th February

Passed out again and I'm not going home yet. Not sure why I passed out last night but when I did I dropped my laptop on the floor and the nurses heard the crash. They rushed me to have another brain scan and the results showed that there was nothing untoward going on. The worst news is that I may have to stay in another night. I can't stand it here, I've never liked hospitals. Let's hope when the doctor comes round, I can convince him that I really am OK to leave.

In the doctor's opinion I just fell asleep. He told me in no uncertain terms, that if I don't rest he will make sure that I have a few more days in here just to make sure I do.

Of course, I promised him that I would, so the news is that I'm going to be discharged in two hours or so, once they've got my medicine ready.

Just got in from the hospital. It was pretty eerie opening the front door after all that's happened, or apparently happened. I'm not certain any longer whether it did happen, but it certainly feels like it was real. Least it's still light. Going to take my pills and rest. Probably have a little read in bed then straight to sleep.

5th February

Slept well last night. Going to email the boss at work and let him know that the doctor's signed me off for a month, then take it easy for the rest of the day.

6th February

NO, NO, NO. It was all meant to be over but it's started again. The time now is 1:15am. About 20 minutes ago I was brought out of my sleep by uncontrollable shivering; the temperature in the flat must be zero now.

The door to the airing cupboard is wide open, and the smells of damp earth and smoke are saturating the air. I can hear the clash of metal on metal and the woomph of fireballs crashing into the ground. I have to see what is going on.

I've only been gone about three hours but it seems like an eternity.

Whether it was stupid or not, all those hours ago I walked straight through that doorway into that unholy land.

Although I want the images and sounds to be gone from my memory I feel I must commit the whole thing to writing before I forget, if I ever will.

Once I was through that gateway to hell I fell to my knees as my legs gave way for no fathomable reason. I ended up belly down next to a familiar pile of rocks.

The legion of Romans (which I had come to the conclusion they were) weren't a legion after all. More like a squad (I don't know the proper name) of about sixty men. From what I could see the battle seemed almost over as the remaining Celts were greatly outnumbered. But just as the final few Britons were about to be subdued a hellish guttural scream pierced the air.

The Roman soldiers paused in their culling of the Celt warriors, being distracted by the noise. The Celts that were left seemed oblivious to this new noise; in fact they seemed to gain strength. They thrust their spears into the bodies of their opponents and followed through with their short swords, slashing and chopping.

Just as the noise reached its peak, hundreds of painted naked warriors appeared over the brim of the hill to my left, carrying more spears, shields, and swords. Now the Romans were in the minority.

Their ranks were reduced easily and most viciously. Some of the Celt warriors not satisfied with the fact that their opponents had died because of their attack, continued to cleave bits from their bodies, in a kind of gleeful mania, eviscerating them as they did so.

Gobbets of human matter were strewn across the dank ground, the earth darkened further as the blood of the defeated soaked into it.

I lay there fixated, paralyzed with the unrelenting horror that was playing out in front of me.

Suddenly one of the Roman soldiers shouted what seemed to be a command and those still standing made a sort of salute to their enemy and put down their weapons. The Celts stopped their onslaught and rounded up the invaders.

Relief crept through me as the tension in my body, a tension I wasn't aware of before, dissipated. I was glad it was over; no person should ever have to witness what I had seen.

A few Celt warriors stood guard around the remnants of the Roman squad whilst the Celtic chieftains discussed something amongst themselves. The discussion finished and one of the Celtic chiefs barked a command to the guards

The Romans were pushed and manhandled into a single line and the chief walked along it as if inspecting them.

When he got to the end he pointed to the third soldier back. A Celt warrior walked up to this man drawing his sword. He stood and faced the soldier eye to eye and raised his sword above his head. The Roman centurion did not move.

The chief barked another command and the warrior brought the sword crashing down onto the centurion's skull slicing it in two.

A cheer went up as the Roman's body collapsed to the ground. The other soldiers in the line charged the Celt warrior, all barring one that is. The first soldier in the line made a break for the open ground. None of the Britons took any notice they were more interested in the final annihilation of the attackers.

I tried not to look, but I felt that if I did not watch then I would be discovered and undergo the same fate.

The centurions managed to kill two more warriors before they were overpowered and sliced from the abdomen to the throat.

One by one the Roman bodies had their mouths sliced open then levered wide for the chieftains to defecate in. Once that abhorrent rite had been completed the soldiers' genitals were carved from their bodies and stuffed into the gaping excrement filled holes.

I was sick to my stomach, needing to retch. I only just kept my silence.

The warriors left and I was alone with the mutilated corpses of Romans and Britons alike.

Then I was back in my flat ready to start this entry. I didn't blink; I don't think I passed out. I was there then here. It's almost as if some incorporeal power was trying to show me something in that land.

Oh god, what sickening memories are being force upon me? What is its purpose? I think I am going to try and rest.

Didn't sleep at all well last night. I'm surprised I'm up and it's still before midday.

Now the phone's bloody ringing.

That was a phone call from the "Sites & Monuments Record Office, County Hall Chelmsford." Janus in fact.

He asked me if I had done what he told me to do during the last phone call. I told him "of course not." He said his spirit guide had revealed as much and this was his reason for calling. He insisted I should follow his instructions from the previous call if I really wanted to put an end to my ordeal.

Anyhow, as I don't think there is anything on this earth that will lead me to the resolution of my problem I am now going to go downstairs to take my shovel from my shed, and wander down the lane to the spot he has directed me to. I have some digging to do.

I couldn't carry out anywhere near as much as Janus has said I should. I'm still weak from the surgery.

One thing though, after two hours of digging, I did get down to some human remains, but I couldn't carry on. The earth was very hard. I will have to carry on tomorrow.

7th February

No disturbances during the night, I'm feeling quite refreshed today actually.

Although what Janus told me yesterday seems utterly ridiculous I'm going to carry on. There's not much else I can do really.

I loaded up my car with the remnants of old furniture I had stored in my shed, stuff I'd decided to take to the tip but never got around to.

Janus had told me that I need to create a pyre, something for the remains to be consumed by. This was all very well but I had no clue as to how I was going to avoid any official questioning of what I was going to do. However, this question did not last in my mind too long because the other choice was much worse. I decided that a spell in prison was worth me performing this rite; the alternative was not worth contemplating.

At the bottom of the lane I unloaded the car and dragged all the craggy furniture to the pit I had dug the other day.

I piled everything up as Janus had instructed and placed the bones I had found on top. Once done I lit the pyre. Thanks to the paraffin the whole lot started to burn.

Within the smoke I thought I caught glimpses of shadowy people flowing towards the sky. Whether this was fact or just another manifestation of my unstable self I have no answer. I was just following Janus's dictate.

It's been a long day, but I can say it's done. Let's hope that's it.

8th February

Another good night's sleep and no evidence that anything malign has gone on.

9th February

Same as yesterday. Can I allow myself to believe that I'll not need to enter anything in this journal ever again?

23rd February

It's been two weeks since I've entered anything in this journal and I hate to say it, Janus seems to have been right.

All those weeks ago he tried to convince me that my ancestors had defiled some Roman invaders after they had surrendered to a greater Celtic army. Were they really my ancestors? I don't know.

He told me that in order to prevent the spirits of my ancient family showing me the whole horror of that time I needed to undo the dead soldiers' defilement; to do this I should give the Roman army's General an appropriate burial with the appropriate rites. Two weeks ago I completed this task.

Found a letter today, in the kitchen, post marked Italy. I seem to remember opening it before and throwing it away, perhaps I didn't. Anyway as it couldn't be for me, not knowing anyone from Italy, I chucked it straight into the bin.

And now we're here, the very last entry in my journal.

Who's going to read it? I don't know. One thing is for sure, I don't want to come back to this journal as its contents chronicle a period of my life I most certainly wish to forget.

THE MACHINES

By Trish Gibbs-Leake

At last I see them
After all these years
Old, dull, metallic, harmless
Yet.... ears pounding,
Hand on my chest
THAT VOICE!
I jerk with every syllable
And clutch my heart.

My daughter sees
With wonder in her eyes
My oldest nightmare on TV
Moving slowly forward
Nowhere to hide
I'm eight again
Reborn
And so are they.

"EXTERMINATE!" they say.

ISBN 1412096227

9 781412 096225